A COWGIRL'S BILLIONAIRE

BARRELS AND HEARTS SERIES BOOK 7

EDITH MACKENZIE

A Cowgirl's Dream (Barrels & Hearts #7):

Images © DepositPhotos – Alan Poulson & Sopotniccy

Cover Design © Designed with Grace

❀ Created with Vellum

This is an ending of sorts, but also a beginning

CHAPTER 1

The popcorn crunched, the saltiness mixing pleasantly with the bourbon Bryce washed it down with. He sat, a sole island, alone in his lavish media room, intently staring at the screen that dominated the opposite wall. The movie panned in to show the side profile of the actress on screen, her blonde hair flying behind her as she urged her horse onward. He pictured her natural auburn hair instead.

"I don't know why everyone has trouble telling them apart. Savannah has always been the more beautiful of the two."

He took another sip of his bourbon, his phone finding its way unbidden into his hand. It would be so easy to call Gabi and get Savannah's number, to hear her sweet voice on the line. Bryce's hand trembled as he battled with himself. No, he couldn't do that to her, no matter how much he wanted it. With a muttered curse, he threw the popcorn, the puffy kernels exploding against the unoffending wall. Drunkenly, he put his face in his hands and sobbed.

~

THE CHICKEN HAWK SPIRALED OVERHEAD, riding the air currents effortlessly. It seemed fiercely independent as it silently glided in the sky. Savannah sighed. Sitting by herself on Travis and Chloe's front porch, it was hard to not feel despondent. She felt like an intruder now that Ash had left. Not that anyone had changed with how they acted toward her, but it felt more like a family she was visiting than her home.

"I thought I might find you out here." Chloe settled down on the step beside her. "You seem to spend a lot of time out here these days. I hope I haven't done anything to upset you?"

Savannah scuffed her boot heel against the wooden stoop. Guilt made her take her time to meet her friend's eyes. "No, I just feel, I don't know, like I'm missing something."

"Or someone."

"Or someone," Savannah agreed. "This is the longest we've ever been apart, and Ash said she's going to be on location for another month and there's no guarantee she'll be home after that."

"You must miss her a lot."

"It's just that I've never really been lonely before. I mean, I have you and everything." She quickly looked at Chloe to make sure she hadn't offended her.

"But I'm not Ash. It's okay. I'd never expect to replace her. The relationship between the two of you is special. Special and loud." Chloe shook her head, laughing. "Actually, I don't think I've ever heard a louder relationship."

"Ash is mainly the loud one."

"I think you both give as good as you get."

Savannah smiled, admitting the truth to what Chloe said. "Maybe. Even in the womb, I think I knew she was there.

And it's not like she's dead or anything, I can still talk to her. But she's not a constant anymore, and I feel off balance with her not around. I know I'll get used to it. I just don't really like the idea of it."

"Maybe, instead of seeing it as losing something, you could see it as gaining an opportunity," Chloe suggested after a moment's silence.

"What do you mean?" Savannah wasn't sure how feeling lonely and blue could be turned into something good, but she was willing to listen. There hadn't been many times where the young Aussie had led her astray. Usually, it was the other way around. Well, it had been when Ash was still there. Savannah felt her eyes burn as homesickness for her twin rose up.

"Well, maybe this is your chance to find out who you are away from Ash. You'll always be a twin, but maybe you could find out who Savannah is."

Savannah stared at the blonde-haired woman, intrigued by the possibility. She and Ash had always been a package deal. From the minute they started elementary school, they had been in the same classes, shared the same friends. Heck when they got their first pony, they'd shared him. She smiled at Chloe, but even she could tell it was a bit quivery.

"Oh, Savannah." Chloe threw an arm around her. "I promise it will get better. I remember when I first moved over here, I missed my mom like crazy. But then you get into a routine and you figure it all out and then it's not so bad. If it makes you feel better, I can always start arguing with you."

"Only if you promise to yell."

Chloe's cornflower blue eyes twinkled. "I'll see what I can do."

~

"CHLOE HAS BEEN DOING a great job with getting the breakers started and some miles on them. Nothing makes a good barrel horse like lots of sweaty saddle blankets." Frankie smiled as she complimented her protégé. Savannah felt like she was at loose ends with Ash gone and the horses they'd bonded with as they hauled them to competitions having all been sold on to new homes. Sure, none of them were going to be world beaters, but their presence had been familiar and comforting. She briefly wondered if she should head back home to where her old horse was in retirement at her parents' home. It might be nice to hang out with him, feed him apples and give him a good brush.

Chloe, obviously misinterpreting her glum expression, was quick to reassure her. "Don't worry, Savannah, there are some really nice ones in the group. I think you'll really enjoy riding the ones that you eventually decide to haul to rodeos."

Savannah smiled, trying to set her friend's mind at ease. "If you're the one that has been doing the training, I'm sure they'll all be nice to ride."

"After what feels like quite a few delays, we are finally making progress on the training facilities at Frankie and Luciano's." Gabi rested her hand on her ever so slightly rounded belly. Seriously, the woman looked like she had just eaten a large lunch, not five months pregnant. "And, drum roll please"—she waited appreciatively as Deb enthusiastically complied—"we are all set to turn the first sod on the building site in two weeks' time." Much excited chatter greeted her announcement. "And that's it for this meeting, unless anyone else wants to add anything."

Deb cleared her throat. Savannah looked at her in interest. It was rare for the tall Australian to take the floor at the meetings Gabi insisted they had. Her style was more to provide a running commentary from the side lines. "I know everyone is keen to get going about their business, especially

Megan and Frankie. But let the Cabrera's enjoy the babies a bit longer." She stood and walked from the room, instructing everyone to wait while she retrieved something. When she returned, she had a large gift bag in her hands. "Megan, we all know that, in a few days, you begin the next exciting part of your life. And although we'll still see you around, you'll have other priorities." Deb paused and looked down at the bag in her hands, appearing to collect her thoughts. "I am, well, we are all bloody proud of you for going to vet school and we wanted to get you something to wish you luck and say we love you." Deb's voice sounded suspiciously gruff as she finished, giving the present to Megan. Savannah was shocked to see tears welling up in her eyes and even more so when she looked at Megan and found her in a similar state.

"Thank you, guys, I'm almost scared to bloody open it if Deb was in charge of shopping." Megan feigned alarm.

"Stop being a galah and open it up," Deb retorted, appearing to have gotten over her emotional turmoil. Megan complied and revealed a snowy white lab coat, its fabric stiff and professional looking, and a shiny stethoscope.

"Thanks, guys. I wondered why Carlos wouldn't let me order these," Megan said.

"Try it on," instructed Gabi. "I want to know if we got the right size."

Savannah watched as everyone fussed over Megan, the group's closeness obvious. It dawned on her that she had never built close female friendships. She had always had Ash and that had been enough for her. Well, maybe it was time. Savannah brushed the nerves away that the thought of putting herself out there brought. It was time to put her big girl pants on.

CHAPTER 2

The rag hit the dirty water in the pail with a satisfying splosh, sending sudsy ripples dancing across its surface. Savannah reached her hand in to retrieve it, wringing out the excess water before returning to wiping down the saddle in front of her.

"I thought I would find you in here." Savannah gave a start at her boss's voice. The act of cleaning the saddlery had been soothing in its monotonous rhythm and her mind had drifted off. Frankie grabbed a tub of leather conditioner and pointed to the pile of gear Savannah had already wiped clean. "Are these ready to be oiled?"

"Yeah, all those are clean. Just need to finish this one before I start." She watched as Frankie pulled up a stool and picked a breastplate out of the mound. Comfortable silence filled the room as the women set to work, their hands busy, but minds free.

"I remember when Megan and Deb and I would do this every time before we went off to a rodeo. They're still some of my best memories." Frankie smiled as she reminisced.

"Yeah, Ash and I would get all our gear ready together

and then make sure we picked different outfits for the weekend so we didn't match." A wave of homesickness for her twin hit her. Determinedly, she swiped at the saddle, fighting against the blurring of her vision.

"It's hard when you're left behind." Frankie's voice was soft and full of understanding.

Her support made the tears tremble on the cusp of falling from her eyes. Savannah dashed at them in frustration. She was acting like Ash had died or something. Her weakness was beginning to make her angry. In fact, she doubted Ash was sitting around mooching and being a big cry baby. "I mean, I'm happy that she's off doing something she loves and all, it's just she used to love going to rodeos." *With me,* she silently added.

"What is it you want to do, Savannah? Is it still rodeos or is it something else? I'd like to think that we've all proven time and again that we support each other no matter what. Look at Chloe only wanting to train, or Megan going to vet school. Heck, look at Ash becoming a movie star."

"It hasn't ever changed for me. I feel it here"—Savannah patted her chest—"as much as I ever have. I want to be a champion. I want to have what you have and I'm not afraid to work for it." She could feel the burn in her soul. The truth ringing in her words left very little doubt she meant them. "I remember seeing you and Delila at the Need for Speed event when I was younger, and I still want that."

"I'm glad to hear that." Frankie chuckled at the memory. "Need for Speed seems like a lifetime ago, but I still feel that burn every time I saddle up. The need to be better, to train harder. But now I want to focus that energy in other ways, to helping others harness that same drive." She set the tub down at her feet and wiped her hands carefully on a clean rag. "Come with me."

Savannah couldn't tell if it was a command or a request,

but it didn't matter. She would do anything this woman asked of her. She'd earned her respect a long time ago, even before they had met. She followed her from the tack room and out into the barn aisle where Chloe was saddling up Nova. The past year of work had filled the filly's frame out nicely. Beneath her buckskin hide, the muscles were clearly defined, twitching to send an annoying fly on its way.

Frankie stopped beside the horse, rubbing Nova on her broad forehead when she nickered in greeting. "From now on, Nova will be your ride. I've been lucky. I had not one, but three horses that helped me get to where I am. They helped me capture my dream and will always be my heart horses. Now it's your turn, and we believe in you. Nova will never be sold, and she's yours to ride for as long as you want to be a partnership. Well, we might need to borrow her from time to time for Carlos to do an embryo transfer." Frankie kissed the buckskin on the nose. "Because I want Nova babies. Chloe's done a lot of the foundation work for you and hauled to a few local events. The rest is going to be up to you. I'm going to give you guys a month to get to know each other, then you start hauling."

Savannah brought a shaky hand up to her forehead, an overwhelming need to sit down. "I don't know what to say." Her voice choked with tears. "Thank you." She rushed forward and hugged Frankie tightly. "Thank you, Frankie, I promise I won't let you down."

Frankie patted her on the back. "Honey, don't worry about me. Just make sure you don't let yourself down. Now, finish saddling up this horse and get out onto that arena. I want to see lots of sweaty saddle blankets before you start hauling."

Savannah gave the Aussie a mock salute. "Aye aye, captain." She set to work, her mind still reeling from the unexpected show of faith and support. She couldn't wait to call Ash and tell her.

IT WASN'T long before Savannah began to wonder if the filly wouldn't have been better named Diva. The spoiled golden princess of Affinity Ranch, she knew she was something special and had the attitude to match. It was beginning to dawn on Savannah that, up until this point, she had somehow managed to avoid working with mares and there may have been a reason for that. Every day, just when she thought she was making progress, Nova would throw in a new challenge that had the cowgirl racking her brains to find a way to address it.

Chloe merely laughed when she told her about her dilemma. "You should be thankful you've never worked with a chestnut mare. If you think Nova's difficult, a redhead is next level." Chloe made a point to stare at Savannah's own luscious auburn locks.

Savannah pulled her trucker hat down a little lower, pretending to ignore her friend's innuendo. "Well, you've had the most to do with her. What am I doing wrong?"

"Look, it's not even what you are or aren't doing wrong with Nova. It's just that she's the type of mare they had in mind when they say 'tell a gelding, ask a stallion, negotiate with a mare'. You can't start bossing her around when she hasn't even decided if she likes you and she's nowhere near trusting you yet."

She mulled her words over, completely lost in what she should do next. Dejected, she began to brush the gleaming buckskin coat. If she couldn't make the mare listen to her, at least she would have the best-groomed horse while she misbehaved. Savannah rested her forehead against Nova's warm neck. In her mind, she could see Frankie and Delila flying around the barrels at the Need for Speed. And then the vision changed, and it was her and Nova. But this time, it was at the Thomas and Mack Center in Las Vegas at the NFR.

"How's she going for you?" The image vanished at Frankie's question.

Savannah pushed away from the mare. "I don't think it's going to work."

Frankie pursed her lips. "What do you mean?"

"Nova and I, we're just not working out. She fights me on everything. Chloe tells me that Nova probably doesn't like me yet." She threw her hands up in the air. "I mean, what am I even meant to do with that piece of information? Try and bribe her with apples? I'm sorry, Frankie, I know I'm letting you down." Savannah couldn't even bear to look her mentor in the face, scared to see the disappointment she knew she would find there. The silence stretched out unbearably until she couldn't take it anymore and she looked up. Frankie had a pensive expression on her face.

"Savannah, have you already ridden, or are you about to?"

"I should have started riding her an hour ago. I'm just stalling."

"Do you mind if I join you?"

Savannah looked at her in surprise. "Sure."

"Cool, I'll go get Sampson. Oh, and don't saddle her up. Just the halter." She watched Frankie walk out of the barn whistling a jaunty tune, unsure what she'd just agreed to.

THE SLENDER blonde sat effortlessly on the big black stallion, each perfectly in sync with the other as they warmed up. It was as if Frankie only had to think what she wanted to happen next and Sampson complied. It was hard not to feel envious of such a harmonious display when Nova swished her tail threateningly, her ears pinned back as she humped along.

"Have I ever told you how I ended up with Sampson?" Frankie asked conversationally.

Savannah grabbed a handful of mane as Nova tensed up beneath her, her head getting concerningly low. "Didn't you get the ride after Delila got hurt?"

"That's part of the story. Senhor Eduardo bred him and he did a good job. Sampson's bloodlines are in the purple on both sides and he's a very handsome boy if I do say so myself." Frankie patted her steed adoringly. The stallion gave a gentle snort in response. *They even appeared to be able to talk to each other,* Savannah thought in despair. *I'm kidding myself if I think I can ever be as good as her.*

"It would have been a great fit too, once Gabi decided she wanted to breed barrel horses."

"Champion Barrel Horses," Savannah corrected, tightening her stomach muscles as Nova surged forward.

Frankie smiled at the correction. "I'm sorry, you're right, Champion Barrel Horses. The thing was that the colt, as they called him back then, couldn't be handled, and Senhor Eduardo thought he was dangerous." Savannah could believe that. There was still a raw power to Sampson, as if it was only contained by the thinnest thread. In fact, she had never seen anyone other than Frankie ride him. "I think I fell in love with this big lug the minute I laid eyes on him and I knew that he deserved a chance. It was only after Luc bought him for me that I got to start working with him. Sure, I'd given him lots of scratches and apples before that, but we only really started to bond once I started training him. The first few months were ugly. Like, I would have thrown the towel in and quit except I'd made such a big deal about him needing a chance that I couldn't admit defeat. So, thanks to stubborn pride, I pushed through it and, little by little, things began to change. I still remember the exact day that I felt he wanted to work with me, not against me." Frankie glanced approvingly at Savannah. "She seems to be going a bit better."

Savannah had been so caught up in Frankie's story that she hadn't even noticed the mare relaxing beneath her as they walked around. "Yeah, but for how long?"

"Nova's a quirky filly. You're not going to be able to train her like the other horses you've worked with. She's going to get bored just working in the arena. She's going to argue when she thinks she's right and, some of the time, she is going to be right. The best horses aren't the ones that are the easiest. They are a breed all to themselves. You need to figure out how to get her to work with you, how she learns, how to become a team. If you can't, you guys will never be the champion team I believe you can be."

CHAPTER 3

The strident ringing tone was monotonous in its regularity as Savannah waited impatiently for her twin to answer. Having triple checked the time difference, she knew she was awake. "Pick up already," she muttered.

"What?" The abrupt answer caught her off guard. Trust Ash to decide to answer at that exact moment.

"Hey, so how have you been?" It felt strange and too formal to speak to her sister like that, but somehow, she was lost with what else to say. Sadly, she realized they were leading different lives now and the easy familiarity that came with always being together was being lost.

"Yeah, busy. I'm in New Zealand now. I think I told you that last time?"

"You did. You were all excited to be in the land of the hobbits."

"Oh my gosh, Savannah, it's so beautiful here. They have beaches that have black sand, and there's even this beach where you can dig a hole and the water is hotter than sitting in a bath. Kirk and I went down just before dawn and picked a spot, dug, and then sat in our own spa on the beach watching the sun rise. It was magic. You should do it sometime."

It was hard not to feel envious. Ash had never talked about traveling the world. She had always been focused on the horses—the same as Savannah. Now, it felt like she was this different person, one that was leaving her behind. "Oh yeah, well, I guess when I save up some money for a vacation, it's something to think about."

"The director I'm working with on this film is great. He's really pushing me and I'm playing this total badarse, but she's really cool. It's a challenge to show her vulnerable side." Ash's enthusiasm flowed through the phone. "Kirk has been a total sweetie and has been working with me to get it just right. I'm not sure what I'm going to do. He leaves to start filming his next one in a few days' time."

"Oh, where is he filming this one?"

"You totally have to tell the girls this—he's filming in a place called Cairns in Australia. It's something to do with modern day pirates and treasure. It's a suspense. He's going to be great in it."

It hadn't escaped Savannah that Ash hadn't once asked how she was going with the horses or rodeos. It stung that Ash was important now and didn't think about it at all. "Well, I have news of my own."

"Savannah, I have to go. They're calling me on set."

"Oh, well I'll be quick. Frankie has given me"—she frowned down at the now dead phone—"the ride on Nova. Not that you care," she whispered, bowing her head in defeat against the sorrow burning in her heart. Savannah almost jumped out of her skin when the phone rang, joy washing away her sadness as she silently berated herself for thinking her sister had deliberately hung up. They must have been disconnected. "Anyway, what I was saying before we got disconnected is that Frankie has given me the ride on Nova."

"That's really good news, but we weren't disconnected." Miranda's unexpected voice sent a jolt of surprise through her.

"Hey, Miranda. Sorry, I was talking to Ash and I think we got disconnected." Savannah nodded to herself. That had to be the explanation. Ash would want to know about Nova. Heck, that filly was the princess of Affinity Ranch.

"Oh." For some reason, Miranda sounded slightly doubtful. "Anyway, you were saying something about Frankie and a Nova?"

Savannah's excitement bubbled up again, Miranda would get it. She was a rodeo girl through and through. "Well, Nova is a who," she began. "Let me start you at the beginning."

"Now, I will do most of the talking with Bryce, so don't worry about any of the negotiations."

Savannah almost had to jog to keep up with Gabi's energetic strides as she crossed the foyer, heading to the elevator. How did the pregnant woman walk so fast? She hadn't really given the negotiations much thought, to be honest. After all, it was Bryce. Savannah felt a warm tingly feeling just thinking about him before realizing she'd fallen behind again and ran to catch up.

For some reason, she'd thought that Bryce would run his business empire from a rustic barn office on a ranch somewhere. Obviously, now that she gave it some serious consideration, it was pretty clear that he would have a corporate headquarters somewhere more metropolitan. Still, the polished skyscraper wasn't what she had in mind when she thought of Bryce.

Gabi tapped her foot agitatedly, staring at the flashing numbers of the elevator display. Smiling eagerly as it chimed, she looked at Savannah, the look of cunning determination almost chilling in its intensity. Savannah had seen glimpses of it before but never in its entirety.

"Let's go get you sponsored."

Savannah trailed silently behind Gabi as they walked through the lobby and approached the receptionist. Everything was tastefully decorated, but it seemed like Bryce had simply signed off on some ideas and handed over his checkbook rather than being actively involved.

"Savannah?" She blinked at Gabi's sharp tone, guessing that her boss had had to repeat herself a few times.

"Um, yes?"

"Linda"—she gestured to the waiting receptionist—"would like to know if you would like something to drink while we're waiting."

"Oh, no thanks, I'm fine." Savannah perched herself on the leather sofa near the large floor-to-ceiling windows, admiring the view below. She wondered if Ash sat in a lot of rooms like this, waiting to speak to casting agents and, well, she wasn't sure who else, but movie type people. She bet she didn't act all jittery and, normally, Savannah didn't either. But her equilibrium felt off lately.

"Ah, Gabi, Savannah. My two favorite gals here to see little ol' me." A thrill went through Savannah as Bryce's booming baritone echoed through the cavernous space. "Y'all come through." Savannah followed Gabi into the room, smiling warmly at Bryce as he held the door open for them— the perfect Texas gentleman.

"Thank you for seeing us today," Gabi said, taking a seat to the immediate left of where, judging from the notepad and pen, Bryce would be sitting. Savannah took the place she was obviously expected to take which, unfortunately, left her sitting the furthest away from Bryce.

"I always worry when you get formal with me, Mrs

Rojas." Bryce sat, immediately beginning to twirl his pen. "Makes me wonder how much this visit is going to cost me." He winked slyly at Savannah. A warm feeling of somehow being in a partnership filled her. "You will have to excuse my PA, Silvia's, absence. She's away sick today. I hope you'll make do with just me."

"I hope Silvia feels better soon and I think we both know investments cost money," Gabi tartly responded. "And I think you'll agree that you will want to get in on the ground floor with Savannah before I find her another major sponsor and you lose her. She is, after all, going to be the world champion in a few years." Savannah almost choked at the statement. No pressure there at all.

Bryce turned sharply assessing eyes to her. "I'm listening. But so far, Savannah hasn't got any major wins at the bigger rodeos."

"That's not down to ability, but rather that we haven't matched her with horseflesh that will take her there. That's about to change." Gabi appeared to be enjoying drawing out her surprise.

"You've found her a new horse?" Bryce raised a questioning brow.

"Not just any horse. Nova. And it was at Frankie's insistence. She thinks Savannah is the one that will continue the legacy of Affinity Stud Ranch. So much so that she has been mentoring her and the filly." Gabi settled back in satisfaction as Bryce digested her news, astutely weighing up the advantages.

"The girl mentored by Frankie Navarro, riding the horse that is bred from the two great horses of her career. That is some serious advertising pull."

Gabi smiled smugly. "I thought you might like it."

"And it's not like Savannah doesn't already have a large collection of Black Angus Western Wear. All we would need to do is send her some of the pieces from our soon-to-be-released collection."

"I see you aren't averse to the idea of sponsoring Savannah."

"I'm not averse to Savannah at all." There was something faintly possessive about the way he looked at her that made her cheeks blush hotly. "I'll write down some numbers and send them your way. I'm sure you'll have something to say about them." Setting his pen down on the table, he stood and extended his hand to Gabi. "As usual, a pleasure doing business with you. I'd thought impending motherhood would soften you, but I'm pleasantly surprised to see it has sharpened your wit, if anything."

"Likewise. Except for the motherhood part." Gabi looked deeply satisfied with the outcome.

Savannah still wasn't sure what had been agreed on as she watched Bryce approach her. He held out his hand and she was surprised to find that it held a business card. "This has my direct number on it. Please, feel free to call me if you want to discuss anything further. I would be more than happy to talk with you in private."

"And I'm sure the paperwork Gabi sends through will have my number on it." At last, Savannah found some of her usual sass. It was satisfying to see the sparkle of admiration in his eyes.

"Touché." Bryce gave a respectful nod of his head.

"And if you have anything further to discuss about sponsorship, it won't be happening in private," Gabi tartly interjected. "I'll give you a follow-up call in a few days to make sure you've received the paperwork I'll be sending over. And if there's nothing further you want to discuss, Savannah needs to get back to the ranch to work Nova." Gabi raised a challenging brow in Bryce's direction, daring him to contradict her.

Bryce gave a wry smile to Gabi. "I wouldn't want to stand in the way of Nova becoming a champion." He turned the full force of his gaze to Savannah. "I look forward, with pleasure, to working with you, Savannah." His words sent a thrill of anticipation up her spine as, much like a mother hen, Gabi began to usher Savannah from the room, leaving nothing but the memory of the promise in his eyes.

CHAPTER 4

Savannah could feel her mouth open and shut like a drowning fish, but dang it if she could stop it. Around her, she could hear people talking, but she didn't have a clue what words they were saying. All she could do was stare at the gleaming Dodge Ram pickup and the behemoth of a horse trailer attached to it.

"Savannah. Savannah?" Deb snapped her fingers in front of the auburn-haired girl's face. "Are you still bloody with us?"

"Do you think she needs to sit down?" Frankie, concerned, began to look around for a convenient chair.

"Well, how do you expect a girl to react when something like this shows up?" Chloe said. "It's enough to make me want to go back on the road."

Savannah missed what Megan said in reply, the image in front of her incredulous eyes blurry as tears welled. "Now you've made her cry," scolded Frankie.

"I can't believe this is mine." Savannah sniffled.

"Well, it's yours as long as you're sponsored by Black Angus," quantified Gabi.

"Don't rain on her parade," muttered Chloe. "Go on, have a sit in it at least."

Savannah shuffled forward, the metal cool and sleek beneath her questing hand. She opened the door and slid into the supple leather of the seat, the steering wheel creaking its newness as she gripped it, the inimitable new car smell assailing her nostrils. She chewed her lip as she recalled an article Ash had read her a few years ago—something about how the smell could actually be toxic if inhaled too much. But Ash was probably off being driven around somewhere in a brand new Rolls Royce or something. Just to spite her twin, she took an extra deep breath. The minute the air hit her lungs, doubt that Ash's article might be true descended over her and she exploded into a coughing fit, attempting to expel as much of the inhaled new car air as she could.

"Bloody heck, now she's choking to death." Deb began to pound her on the shoulder, which only compounded the situation as it knocked more air from her lungs.

"When you're quite finished, maybe you should check out the trailer," Gabi said dryly with a long-suffering expression. "Seriously, you're just turning into a more argumentative version of Frankie. I know you idolize her and all that, but you might be taking it a bit far." Frankie gave her friend a wounded look.

"Come on, Savannah. I'm dying to see what a rig this flash looks like inside." Chloe walked around to the door of the horse trailer, waiting for her friend to follow.

"I'd be happy as a pig in mud if this rig was mine," Deb agreed. "Not carrying on like a pork chop."

If the new pickup truck had overwhelmed Savannah, it was nothing compared to the horse trailer. A gleaming thirty-three feet long of steel perfection and, in perfect eight-inch-high lettering, her name. The horse area was state of the art, ensuring Nova would have a smooth and, most importantly, safe ride to rodeos. But inside, well, inside was where Savannah's bottom lip began to tremble again.

"Oh, geeze. Someone better bloody get some tissues in here," Deb grumbled. "She's about to ruin the upholstery."

~

"It has two pop-outs, one in the main living area with a sofa that folds into a bed and dining table, along with a kitchen. The second pop-out is for another bedroom. I could hardly believe my eyes. The trailer has two queen sized bedrooms in it! Two. Queen. Sized. Bedrooms. Ash!" Savannah stared at her twin's face on her computer screen. "Tomorrow, I'll take a video and give you the grand tour."

"I guess I'll need to come back for the maiden voyage. You know, help you break it in."

"Hmm, no, never again." Savannah began to shake her head emphatically at her sister's suggestion.

"I think you're remembering it as much worse than it was." Ash held a hand to her heart. "I've matured since we last shared a space anyway."

"Nope, I don't think so. You're very messy and I can't see that changing at all."

"Well, then it's a good thing I'm too busy to come back anyway."

Savannah tried not to let it show how much her sister's sudden rejection hurt. She'd been secretly excited that she might get to see Ash soon. It felt like ages since she'd last seen her. "Well, that's good then. I didn't want to have to hang out with you anyway."

"Good." Ash scrunched up her face and poked her tongue out. "I need to go have a shower and start getting ready. It's my day off and Kirk has flown across from Australia for the day just so we can have lunch together. Say hello to everyone for me."

Savannah farewelled her sister and stared at the screen long after it had gone blank. Would she ever get used to being apart from her twin?

～

NONE OF IT SEEMED RIGHT. The drive to a rodeo ground she had never been to—the furthest she'd ever driven for one—the new rig and, sure as heck, sitting at a table in her fancy horse trailer eating her dinner alone. She pushed her food around on her plate, a hollow feeling in her chest and a lump in her throat that never seemed to go away these days.

"Savannah, are you in there?" Miranda's voice called from outside.

"Come on in." Savannah pushed her plate away, giving up on getting her appetite back.

"Geeze, I wouldn't have thought that this big rig was yours—except that it has your name all over it," marveled Miranda. "I guess Black Angus is really pulling out all the stops to look after their new sponsored rider."

"Yeah, I'm pretty lucky." Savannah stood and took her dishes to the sink.

"You don't sound like you feel lucky." Miranda peered at her.

"I don't know how to describe how I feel without sounding ungrateful." Savannah chewed on the inside of her cheek, trying to keep her emotions in check.

"I'm your friend. Tell me what's wrong." Miranda smiled reassuringly. "Maybe I might be able to help?"

Gratitude for her friend's unconditional support made her smile. "Okay, well I've never done any of this by myself before. I'm nervous and scared that I'm going to let Frankie down—not to mention Bryce with his sponsorship. I'm still not even sure if Nova likes me."

"From where I stand"—she smiled—"or sit, as the case might be, all I see is a tough, crazy barrel racer."

Miranda's words put the steel back into Savannah's spine. "Heck yeah. We're tough cowgirls and totally got this."

Her friend smiled for a moment, her expression unreadable. "That's my girl."

CHAPTER 5

The bite of the metal as it hit her shin made Savannah grit her teeth against the pain. It turned into a grimace as she heard the hollow thud of the barrel hitting the sand. "I swear you like making me pick these things up," teased Chloe as she jumped off the arena fence and sauntered across the sand to set it right again.

"Well, I wouldn't want you to get bored sitting over there." Savannah rubbed at her leg, the filly still dancing, wanting to run. Typical Nova having no intention of listening to her, just fighting for her own way. She knew Frankie had told her that she needed to find a way to work with the buckskin, but she was fast approaching the end of her tether as far as ideas and patience go. Heck, this time back at the ranch was meant to give both her and the filly a chance to recharge their batteries, but all it did was tighten the anxiety and mounting frustration in her chest. It hadn't exactly made her feel better when Frankie had walked out of their training session. It appeared that even her mentor knew when something was beyond hope.

Glumly, she circled Nova, trying not to succumb to

despair. "Look out. Looks like Frankie has decided to come out and play," Chloe said from the sidelines. Savannah turned to see the Aussie cowgirl mounted on the gorgeous black Sampson. There was something about the sight that made her feel even worse. The champion cowgirl mounted on her world-famous horse and her, a nobody with a horse everyone agreed had talent but she couldn't bring it out.

"I've been busy and, between the twins and breeding season, I haven't had a chance to ride him since last time we worked the horses together." Frankie spoke easily, as if to someone that was of the same caliber of her. It was something that Savannah had always admired. There wasn't a better horsewoman than Frankie. She was a world champion and, while she wore the mantle of all that easily, it hadn't changed who she was at her core.

"Well, not much has changed with Nova and I since we last rode together." It pained Savannah to admit it.

"From where I sit, a lot has changed. You've gone out on the road together and dealt with that as a team. I mean, she has had plenty of opportunity to ditch you in the sand and she hasn't." Savannah had to smile her agreement at the last comment. It was true. She wouldn't put it past the buckskin to get rid of her if she really didn't want to be ridden. "But what is the biggest change is this chip on your shoulders I'm seeing. All of your frustrations are leveled at what Nova is doing or not doing. You might need to take a step back and look at what you're doing."

Savannah felt like she'd been slapped. She felt her features go slack with surprise and then anger. She had been doing everything she could to get Nova going well.

Frankie raised her hand to stall any protests. "I think maybe we should swap horses for a while today."

A thrill shot through Savannah as she eyed the powerful stallion. This was a once in a lifetime opportunity she wasn't going to miss out on. She couldn't remember ever seeing anyone else ride Sampson except for Frankie. Quickly, she swung down from the saddle, ready for the swap. Effortlessly Frankie did the same before handing her the reins.

"Just remember, I know this horse inside and out. He will tell me exactly what you aren't or are doing up there. Just move him around so the two of you get used to each other."

Sampson was incredibly sensitive to her aids. Savannah had never ridden a horse that was so highly trained. It was electrifying. Out of the corner of her eye, she could see Frankie quietly working Nova. Her manner was calm as she asked the filly to go through her paces, turning her one way and then the other. The buckskin's tail stopped swishing and her expression gradually softened, her ears bobbing gently with each stride. Finally, Frankie deemed the filly had done enough and pulled her to a halt. Savannah reached down and patted Sampson on the neck as he did the same. "Good boy."

"Now that you've gotten to know each other, I want you to run the barrels." Frankie sat easily in the saddle, as if her suggestion hadn't just made Savannah's heart start pounding.

"Like, now?" Her mouth was dry, making the words stick.

"Now."

Savannah gathered up the reins, wishing her nerves were so easily collected. Taking a deep breath, she set her heels against Sampson's sides. The great horse sprung forward, his acceleration rapid. As she lined up the first drum, she felt the exact moment he switched off from listening to her and took control. That's not to say he didn't do everything right, but she was simply relegated to the role of passenger and remained so for the rest of the pattern, Sampson running the barrels foot perfect with no input from her.

Frankie laughed at her when she pulled up, shellshocked. "I'm not even sure how to describe what happened."

"He doesn't trust you to take care of him, so he decided to

take care of you instead." Frankie smiled fondly at her equine partner. "That was always his biggest trait and the one that got him tarred as being dangerous. Once I got him to trust me 100%, he was putty in my hands and that's the reason I was able to train him to the level he is." She rubbed Nova's neck. "Now, I think we should have a little go." She put her legs on, the filly leaping away. Savannah quickly turned the prancing Sampson around so she could watch.

Nova flew across the sand like she had wings on her heels. She had the power of her sire, but she combined it with a gracefulness that was spellbinding to see. As they approached the first barrel, she waited for Frankie to sit deep and take a pull. Instead, the Aussie cowgirl sat quietly in the saddle, simply sitting a little deeper. Nova began to check her speed, waiting. Savannah held her breath, and Frankie leaned into the turn guiding her smoothly around it. The buckskin's haunches bunched, digging into the sand. As they came out of the turn, her ears were pricked, seeking out the next drum. Savannah felt like she was watching a completely different horse. One that was a champion. The sting of humiliation burned her eyes as she watched the pair complete the course and return.

"I can't get her to do it like that," she admitted, wanting to cry. Who was she kidding? She was never going to be in the same league as Frankie.

"That's because you are so busy henpecking at everything she's doing wrong that you aren't letting her do what she can do right. She isn't going to try if she is always getting picked on. She's just not that sort of horse." Frankie slid from the saddle and held the reins out. "Now I want you to do it. This time, just do it to enjoy it."

Reluctantly, Savannah slid from Sampson's back and approached the filly. When was the last time she'd ridden simply to enjoy it? The closest was when she'd last ridden the horses bareback with Frankie but, even then, it had felt like she'd had something to prove. She swung herself up into the saddle. She knew that she'd felt like Nova had something to prove every time she sat on her. She patted Nova on the neck, suddenly conscious of the tension in the way the filly held herself. "Come on, girl, let's have some fun."

Savannah felt the hesitation in her horse and then she put her legs on, asking her to go forward. After a split second, Nova responded. The pattern they ran was by no means perfect, but there was a freedom that hadn't been there before, a tentative step toward a bond. Her jaw that she hadn't even known she had been clenching for months now loosened and it felt good. Wanting to be a champion was all well and good, but maybe she might just start concentrating on enjoying the journey instead.

CHAPTER 6

Machinery boomed and crashed, the smell of wet concrete and welding all around as Savannah trailed at the end of the little group, trying to take in every detail. It was hard not to get caught up in the pride radiating off Frankie and Luciano as they gave a tour of the construction site that was currently their ranch. Savannah couldn't believe just how big it was going to be upon completion. Heck, a body could get lost in there. Judging from the faces around her, she wasn't the only one who was awed by the sight.

"This is what happens when you leave Gabi in charge of the planning," Deb whispered to Megan, who was busy trying to stop Edward from toddling off toward the jagged pieces of piping sticking out of a wall.

"You know I can hear you." Gabi didn't even bother turning her head to address her accusers.

"Gracie, don't run too far ahead," Frankie called after the girl. "Your mother will kill me if you get hurt."

"Nah, she's made of tough stuff. Just like her mom," Mitch said proudly.

"We still have to complete a lot of the work, but I think you can start to see what the finished facilities will look like." Luciano puffed his chest out proudly as he spoke, his arm around his wife. It was a lovely sight, especially given the fact that he had a baby carrier strapped to both his chest and back carrying the twins.

"Am I too late for the tour?" Savannah turned in surprise at Bryce's voice.

"We've only just started." Frankie smiled warmly in welcome at her long-term sponsor and friend.

Bryce fell into place beside Savannah as the group proceeded. The undercover arena was immense with spectator seating on three sides. Separated by a laneway were two large barns and then extra yards to hold another fifty horses. There were also amenity blocks for visitors. Savannah had been under the impression that Frankie was building some facilities for clinics, but this was something else. This was a full equine complex.

By the time they made it back to where they'd started, Savannah was beginning to feel the first pangs of hunger. She discreetly glanced down at her watch and, seeing the time, began to appreciate why her belly was grumbling.

"If you don't have any dinner plans, I would enjoy your company. That is, if I can interest you in grabbing a quick bite to eat." Savannah looked up in surprise to see Bryce was talking to her. The rest of the group had grown silent as they raptly waited for her reply.

"I'm starving," she said as her belly let out another very unladylike gurgle.

Bryce threw his head back and laughed appreciatively. Maybe it was the fresh air or perhaps it was the company, but Savannah couldn't help thinking he looked years younger out here, away from his fancy high-rise.

"Well, judging from the noises your belly is making, we'd best hurry before you fade away."

"Let me go home first and wash some of this ranch smell off me and I'll meet you there." Savannah was suddenly conscious that she had a very livestock odor about her.

"I think you are fine, but I have learned in life to never argue with a lady. How about I text you through the place to meet?"

"I think that'll work. Unless any of y'all have a better idea?" Savannah turned to ask the agog group at large. Suddenly everyone was busy looking elsewhere. She smiled up at Bryce. "I think that's a yes."

"Good, I'll walk you to your car." He held his arm out expectantly. Self-consciously, she accepted feeling the stare of the others drilling into her back. Bryce could obviously feel it too as he leaned in a bit closer. "Let them stare."

It was only a short walk to where everyone had parked up. Bryce nodded at Savannah's new Dodge Ram. "How are you liking it?"

"It's great. I've never had a brand new car before. Heck, I've never had a slightly old car. I can't thank you enough for it."

"Well, technically, it's from the company. But I wanted you to have the best to drive around in." He smiled fondly at his sportscar, which appeared small compared to her pickup truck. "I have to admit cars are a bit of weakness for me, I just bought this one last week."

Savannah looked closer at the bright yellow sportscar. Its badge looked unfamiliar. "What is it?"

"It's a McLaren P1. I've wanted one for a while, but it came down to two reasons that finally got me over the line to buy it." Bryce wiped some dust off the wing mirror with his sleeve.

"Oh, what are those?"

"Well, it's a hybrid supercar, so I like to feel I'm doing my bit as I cruise down the freeway at insanely fast speeds."

Savannah couldn't help but be impressed with his concern for the environment, even if it was tempered with a need to go fast. "What's the second?"

"The doors lift up." She burst out laughing, waiting for him to give her the real reason. When she realized he was dead serious, her amusement only increased. Bryce looked wounded by her laughter. "Seriously, check it out." He pressed a button and both of the doors lifted vertically up into the air. "You have to admit, it's pretty cool and worth every bit I paid for it."

"Was it expensive?" Savannah couldn't fathom buying a car just because it had fancy doors.

"This one cost just over two million dollars, but I've seen them go for a lot more. I bought it because I wanted it, but it's also a good investment." Bryce grinned at her and Savannah realized her mouth was open in shock. She took a few steps away from the car, scared she might damage it. She also made a mental note to make sure he drove away first. There was no way her insurance would cover it if she damaged that car.

"Well, I'd better get going if I want to be cleaned up and changed before I starve to death." Savannah jingled her keys nervously in her hands.

"If you like, I can pick you up for dinner?"

The thought of sitting in that car terrified her. "Um, it's okay. I'll meet you there."

Bryce slid into the sleek leather seat and fired the ignition, the car purring to life. "Don't keep me waiting too long," he said. "I have quite an appetite."

~

By the time Savannah arrived at the cute little restaurant she'd suggested, Bryce already had two empty glasses in front of him and was in the process of finishing a third. Peeking at him from beneath lowered eyelashes as she hung her jacket on the back of her chair, she decided he didn't appear drunk, just comfortably relaxed.

"I hope I didn't keep you waiting too long," she said by way of greeting. Bryce stood and held out her chair with a little flourish, making her giggle. Delectable aromas wafted out from the kitchen that was fully open to the customer's view.

"I would wait an eternity for a beautiful lady," Bryce flirted as he settled her into her seat before taking his own. Her knees bumped against his under the table. Self-consciously, she shifted them away, hoping he wouldn't notice her clumsiness. The hint of a smile on his face told her otherwise, but Bryce didn't look like he minded their physical closeness at all. The knowledge sent a frisson of excitement up her spine. "I've taken the liberty of ordering us some starters while I was waiting. I hope you like tater skins and buffalo wings?"

"Do I ever. In fact, that's what I normally order—when Ash and I used to come here." It came as a shock to Savannah that she didn't feel the usual sadness when she thought of her sister.

"Don't tell anyone, but I've driven past this place quite a few times over the years and I've never stopped in once." He leaned in closer, glancing around to make sure no one could hear. "It looked a bit like a biker's bar from the outside." Savannah giggled, picturing Bryce with his fancy car parked up beside a long row of Harleys. "I think I'm about to become a regular." Bryce drained his glass and held up a hand to signal the waitress to order another one.

"I won't tell if you don't." Savannah was beginning to

worry that Bryce was drinking because of her company. Anxiously, she searched for some small talk. "What made you decide to start Black Angus? Was it something your parents did?"

Bryce waited while the waitress set down his fresh drink and cleared the empty glasses. "My parents were very working class, but then my dad got sick and, with all the medical bills, we lost everything."

She reached out to clasp his hand in sympathy. "Oh, Bryce, that's horrible."

He sniffed, his face drawn into grim lines. "It wasn't exactly great at the time. Anyway, it turned out I was a born hustler. I had a knack for turning one dollar into five dollars, sometimes even fifty." He shrugged, a wry smile on his lips. "And I guess that never changed. I first started out buying hats and shaping them to customers, and then I started getting my friend's mom to sew shirts for me to sell at a little market stall. Somehow, I managed to talk a bank into lending me some money and, next thing, I had a shopfront and Black Angus Western Wear was born." He took a sip of his drink. "But I've kept hustling, even with it doing well. One thing I'm really passionate about is something my friend, Colt Montgomery—you might have heard of him? He's a roper?"

"Um, you mean the world champion roper?"

"Yeah, that's him. Anyway, he and I invested in this little start-up company for green energy that created this solar paint. It's dandy. You paint it on anything, and it'll harvest the energy of the sun." Savannah loved how Bryce's eyes sparkled with his enthusiasm as he spoke.

"So, you could paint it on a car, and it could run off the energy it created?"

"Harvested," he corrected, taking another drink. "Ah, here are our starters," he said as the waitress set down the dishes. "Would you like to order now?"

"I'm good to order if you are."

"I'll have the steak, rare. And the lady would like?" Bryce raised a brow in query.

Savannah smiled at the waitress. "Can you please make that two steaks, rare, thanks." She waited while the waitress removed their menus and then took a bite of one of the tater skins. "Man, I love these."

"I was just about to say the same thing about these buffalo wings." Bryce licked his fingers, smacking his lips in appreciation. "It's a good thing my date suggested coming here."

Savannah could feel herself blush. She hadn't been sure if this counted as a date or not. "You were saying you invested in solar paint," she prompted.

"I was. Anyway, it's been doing great. And then another friend needed a partner with money to start up a recording label, and another needed funding for a movie production company. All these people are crazy talented, and they've gone on to be hugely successful and, by default, I have too." Savannah felt a connection buzzing between them as he opened up to her. "The best thing about money isn't the cool things you can buy and, believe me, there's plenty."

Savannah giggled. "Like cars that have doors that open up."

He winked at her. "There's that. But the thing that I would miss the most if it all disappeared tomorrow is being in a position to help people. There's something about the thrill you get from it. I've never experienced it when I've done anything else and believe me, I've done some crazy things."

Curiosity burned brightly through Savannah, her imagination on fire. "Like what?"

"Well, have you ever had dinner on an iceberg while you watched the Northern Lights overhead? It's the closest to God I've ever felt." Savannah stared at him, not even able to fathom what that experience had been like. "Then there was that time I got obsessed with that Titanic movie—you know the one that has that song."

"I know the movie."

"Well, I was bidding on some cutlery they'd salvaged from the wreck and I thought, 'this is stupid, wouldn't it be a lot cooler to go and see the titanic?' So, I had Silvia—" He paused to take a drink. "Silvia's been working for me for a while. At this stage in our professional relationship, I have my suspicions she might have worked for the FBI previously. Anyway, she made some phone calls and the next thing I know, I'm on this mini submarine thing and going down to where it gets really freaky and dark. You can't see anything except what's lit up by the spotlights and then, there she was. The Titanic."

Savannah shook her head, unable to process how one went about arranging it. "You've seen the Titanic?"

"Yeah. That's the other great thing about money—the experiences you can have. I'm pretty sure I could get on that rocket that's planned to go to Mars if I really wanted to."

"Don't you dare."

He laughed at her bossy tone and then a shadow fell over his face. "But it's come at a cost." Bryce drained his glass and held up a hand yet again for a refill.

Savannah was becoming increasingly concerned with how much alcohol he was consuming. He didn't appear tipsy, just introspective. But based on how much he'd drunk since she'd taken a seat, he had to be a lot drunker than he seemed. His eyes were sad as he stared down into the empty glass in his hands. "I was so busy all the time, scared that I would lose everything like Dad did, focused on making money that I made a terrible boyfriend."

Although she hadn't known him as long as the others, she couldn't remember him ever having a girlfriend. "I'm sure you weren't that bad."

"She was the closest I've ever come to being in love. I used to call her my snow lily, she had the most beautiful pale skin and it seemed perfect for her. Her name was Lily Snowden."

"She sounds beautiful." Savannah wasn't sure why the mood at the table had turned so dark. The hairs on the back of her neck began to stand on end.

"I'd only just started Black Angus when we first got together and, if I'm honest, I knew she loved me. It wasn't that I didn't care about her, I did, but I was just never there. Maybe if I had been, I'd have seen the signs. Maybe I could have done something."

Savannah was beginning to get a horrible sick feeling in her stomach. "What happened?"

The bleakness in his usually happy eyes scared her. "I came home one day to a note saying goodbye. I thought she meant we were over, that she'd finally had enough. It never entered my mind that it could mean anything more."

Savannah couldn't stop staring at Bryce, a horrifying certainty beginning to form in her mind. "But it did, didn't it." It was more of a statement than question.

He nodded, bowed under his own guilt. "A couple of days later, her parents turned up on my doorstep, disheveled, screaming at me—how could I do this to their baby? What sort of monster was I? They'd found her car parked near a bridge and, a few days later, they'd pulled her body from the water."

Savannah was stunned into silence at the tragic ending. Bryce drained the drink the waitress had only just set in front of him. The rest of the evening, neither of them barely touched their food and Bryce continued to drink heavily. Finally, Savannah had had enough and asked for the check, which a very drunk Bryce paid for.

"Come on, Romeo. It's time to head home. Now, where did you park?"

"A gentleman should walk the lady to her car." Bryce slurred the words.

"I don't think you're in any position to drive anywhere, and since I'm pretty confident your car is worth a whole lot more than mine—actually, scratch that. I know your car is worth about thirty Dodge Rams. I'm going to leave mine here and drive yours and, frankly, the idea of that terrifies me."

"You just want to come home with me." He blinked at her owlishly, making her giggle.

"No, you're coming home with me," she said, holding her hands out for his car keys.

"If the lady insists." He promptly stumbled over the curb on the way to getting into the passenger side.

Palms sweating, Savannah tried to get herself into a comfortable position to take control of something worth more than she'd make in her lifetime. She sighed. Well, wasn't this the first date every girl dreamed of.

TRAVIS PLACED Bryce none too gently on the sofa. "He's gonna have one heck of a headache when he wakes up in the morning."

Savannah covered his prone body gently with a blanket. "I don't think it will be the first one for him." She brushed some hair out of his face, her heart breaking for the pain she never knew he carried around, hidden behind the kind, genteel façade. "And I don't think it'll be the last.

CHAPTER 7

The groans and cussing emanating from the living room suggested that Bryce had woken up in the exact condition Travis had predicted. Savannah turned the bacon before pouring two mugs of coffee. Her hand hovered over the sugar pot indecisively before dumping two heaped spoonfuls into the mug destined for Bryce. Heavy footsteps preceded the suffering man as he stumbled into the kitchen looking like a bear with a very sore head. He quickly shielded bloodshot eyes from the bright mid-morning sun streaming into the room.

Frankly, Savannah was impressed the man was even able to stand given how much he'd consumed last night. She held out the mug of coffee. "I didn't know how you liked it."

"Black will do just fine," he mumbled, sinking into a chair, holding his head. Savannah loaded the plates up with eggs and bacon and headed back to the table, sitting opposite him.

"I'd ask how you feel this morning, but it's pretty obvious."

"Savannah, I only have hazy recollections from last night and I don't even remember getting here. Please tell me I didn't do or say anything that would jeopardize our friendship or embarrass myself too much." He squinted painfully at her, a world of misery in the tortured depths of his eyes.

Savannah winced just looking at his eyes. She could only imagine what it must feel like for Bryce. She loaded up her fork. "Eat up before your food gets cold."

Bryce didn't move. "You haven't told me anything about the missing pieces from last night yet."

Her fork gave a slight clink as she set it down on her plate. "You didn't embarrass yourself. Yes, you drank more than you should have, and that's why I brought you back here. Which reminds me, Travis will be back soon to take me to pick my car up."

After a moment, he took hold of his fork, pensively stabbing at the food on his plate. "I remember talking about starting the business."

"If you're asking if you told me about Lily, the answer is yes." Bryce stilled. Savannah touched his hand gently. "I won't tell anyone what you told me, but Bryce, if you ever want to talk or something, I'm here, anytime."

"Thank you, Savannah, that's very kind of you." Somehow, the way he said it made her doubt that he would. It didn't surprise her when he left not long after, his food untouched.

ALL CONVERSATION CEASED OR, more to the point, all activity came to a standstill as soon as Savannah stepped into the barn. Chloe stopped saddling her horse to stare at her, Deb materialized at the top of the bunkhouse stairs, and Frankie and Gabi appeared to be making as rapid a progress from the Cabrera's house as the heavily pregnant Gabi could achieve.

For a moment, Savannah had the overwhelming urge to

run before her interrogation could begin. It did surprise her a little that Frankie and Gabi made it to the barn before Deb had reached the final step of the stairs.

"I just about died when I woke up this morning and Travis told me Bryce was asleep on our sofa," Chloe cried.

"I bet it wasn't the bloody ending Bryce had in mind for the first date." Deb chuckled.

"It wasn't a date," corrected Savannah.

"We all heard him ask you out," Gabi said. "And as your manager, I should have advised against muddying the waters with going on a date with your major sponsor."

"One that ended with him snoring on your couch," Deb added, wiggling her eyebrows suggestively.

Savannah ground her teeth so fiercely in frustration that she worried she might have taken out a filling. Darn it, how many times did she have to say it wasn't a date? Or was it? Bryce had mentioned it was a date but, if it was, it hadn't exactly been a good one. He'd opened up to her, but he had admitted he didn't even remember most of it and it had ended with him being so drunk he'd passed out on her couch.

"Did I miss the recap of the date?" Megan waltzed into the barn. "I can't stay too long. I haven't even stopped to see Edward yet."

"He's fine. I just saw him when I dropped the twins off to visit Nanny Ana and Poppy Eduardo," Frankie said. "But how were your practice exams today? Do you think you'll be ready for the real thing?"

Savannah heaved a mental sigh, relieved the focus had shifted from her. Quietly, she grabbed a halter and headed out to collect Nova. At least the filly wasn't causing her as much aggravation as her friends lately.

CHAPTER 8

Chloe climbed down from the ladder at the back of the trailer where she had just secured the last of the hay. "I think that should be more than enough to last you." She brushed her hands on her jeans. "And if it isn't, too bad. I'm absolutely buggered from getting it up there."

Savannah laughed. "Well you did ask if there was anything you could help me with. But thank you, I'm glad I didn't have to do it." She felt lightheaded, excited. Somehow, a weight had been lifted off her and she was laser-focused on getting on the road and showing what Nova was capable of. It was night and day to how she'd felt the last time she had loaded up.

"Well, if your majesty is done with my services, I think I'll go have lunch. You gonna join me?"

The shrill ring of her phone made her jump. "I'll be there in a minute." Savannah reached into her pocket to retrieve it. Seeing Miranda's name flashing on the screen she answered. "Hello, all ready to hit some rodeos?"

"That's what I was calling to talk to you about. I'm having some issues with my truck and I was wondering if I could haul with you for a while? Just till I can get some money together to get my rig fixed," she added quickly.

"Heck yeah. I'd love the company. You know, the second bedroom in this thing hasn't even been used yet. I'm planning on leaving here first thing tomorrow morning. I should be at your place by lunchtime."

"You're an angel. I'll have everything ready." Miranda sounded as excited as Savannah felt. It was going to be so much fun having someone to share the road with again.

"See you then." She hung up and headed into the barn. She hadn't felt this motivated to compete in ages. She rubbed her hands together gleefully. This was going to be one heck of a trip.

Savannah sat down in the saddle, lowering her weight, asking Nova to check her speed. The filly responded, shifting her center of gravity lower as she prepared to turn. The run had been quick around the first two drums, the buckskin trying hard. At the last minute, Savannah felt Nova drop her shoulder in, cutting the line too close. The sting of metal biting into her shin was followed, as if in slow motion, by the barrel wobbling like a drunk out on the town. She urged the mare away, straightening up for the finish line, praying it would stay standing. Quickly, she risked a glance over her shoulder and watched in frustration as it toppled over. A quick look at the time added to her disappointment. If she hadn't knocked down that barrel, her time would have been fast enough to be in the money.

She took a pull on the reins and gave Nova's lathered neck a pat. "You were a good girl. Next time, I'll set you up better, I promise." The filly let out a long snort as if agreeing.

Miranda jogged her mare over from where she'd been cooling him down. "I thought you had that one."

"Me, too. But I couldn't ask for more. She tried the whole time and I think that last drum was a miscommunication on my part. I thought she had it and she was waiting for me." She patted her horse again. "Good girl, Nova. We'll get there yet."

"Well, after that run, I think we need to have a drink to commiserate."

"Or celebrate," Savannah corrected her as she halted Nova to wait for a cowboy warming up for the next event to pass on his horse.

Miranda gave her an odd look. "Or celebrate knocking a drum, if that's what you want to do."

Savannah smiled happily at her. "That's exactly what I want to do."

SAVANNAH HANDED the beer to Miranda and joined her on the sofa to watch the reality show that was on the TV. There was something to being able to relax with a cold brew in the comfort of your own space that she'd never fully appreciated before. The old trailer she'd shared with Ash had been smelly and cramped, not aided by the fact that her sister had a tendency to spread her stuff everywhere. She clinked her bottle to Miranda's in salute. Yep, her new traveling buddy was an improvement.

She glanced down to see she had a new message from Bryce asking how she'd performed. Savannah wasn't sure if he was asking as a friend, as someone more, or as her sponsor.

"You look like you just got in trouble," Miranda said with a laugh, making her face scrunch up in an imitation.

"No, well not really. I just don't know how to answer it is all."

Miranda snatched the phone from her hand and read the message before Savannah could stop her. "Bryce? Is this Bryce your sponsor?"

Savannah had forgotten she hadn't filled her friend in on the disastrous date. "Yeah, he sponsors me. But we also kinda went on a date."

"What! Didn't your manager tell you that you don't have to do that sort of thing these days? In fact, I don't think it's very politically correct that you had to do it."

Savannah blinked at her, momentarily confused with the tangent she'd gone on. "Oh! No, it's nothing like that. I wanted to go on it, and it wasn't really a date—or at least much of one. I would've gone even if he wasn't my sponsor."

"Okay, then what's the problem? Just tell him what happened and then we can get back to girl time and chilling."

"Well, I don't want to tell him I didn't do that great. It's getting a bit embarrassing that I haven't had a winning or at least a placing run yet." She didn't add that she wasn't sure how personal the message was.

"Then ignore it."

Savannah was horrified at her friend's callous disregard. "I'm not going to do that. I just need to figure out what to say." *And how to say it.*

AFTER THAT FIRST initial message and rather vague response, it was like some sort of floodgate opened. Bryce would send through texts that, during the day, were articulate and often quite witty. It was the long, rambling ones that were often sent at odd hours of the night that began to make Savannah suspect that Bryce's drinking problem went further than their disastrous date. There was no escaping the fact that he was an alcoholic—a high-functioning one, but an alcoholic, nonetheless.

Nova continued to improve. Savannah found that she was beginning to know what mood the filly was in just by looking at her and tried to ride accordingly. That night was the biggest rodeo she was riding in yet, and it didn't help that Bryce had told her that he'd be there.

As they walked to the arena, Nova felt electric. Her strides short and energized like a tightly coiled spring ready to be released. Previously, Savannah would have tried to hold her in, fighting to control it. But now she knew to let the filly be, to give her the freedom to keep moving.

"Competitor two three one, you're next."

Savannah nodded at the steward, aware that her smile felt a little too tight on her face, the skin a little too drawn. She closed her eyes and turned her thoughts inward for the briefest of moments. *Trust in Nova and let her trust you.* The words became a mantra as she breathed in and out, harnessing her nerves into a tight focus on the job at hand. The gate to the alley swung open and, beneath her, Nova's legs began a staccato tempo like pistons under pressure. Savannah leaned forward and the cowgirl and horse sprung forward, come what may, as one entity.

"I believe congratulations are in order." Bryce rested his hand easily on the small of Savannah's back.

A shiver ran deliciously up her spine from where she could feel the warmth of his large hand through the fabric of her top. She couldn't contain her grin. She felt rejuvenated and giddy. "Nova was such a good girl and for this to be our first win at an event like this"—she gestured around her —"I'm ecstatic."

"From what I saw, it was a good ride from a very competitive looking partnership." For the first time, Savannah realized that Bryce had brought someone with him. Flustered under the stranger's praise, she smiled at him in thanks.

"Savannah, this is my friend, Colt Montgomery. Colt, this is Savannah and her friend Miranda." Bryce, ever the gentleman, gallantly introduced them.

"Ma'am, it sure is a pleasure after all I've heard about you. Bryce tells me you might—just might—be the next Frankie." Colt doffed his hat to Miranda. "Pleasure to meet you, too. Bryce didn't tell me that Savannah had such a pretty friend."

Savannah watched, gobsmacked, as Miranda simpered up at him. For some reason, her friend's manner struck her as fake. Bryce had obviously been watching the pair as well. At his wink, she immediately realized the two were in cohorts and Bryce had brought Colt along as his wingman.

"Subtle." Savannah congratulated him.

"I'm glad you like it. Miranda made quite an impression on me last time and I knew that if I wanted to spend some quality time with my number one gal, I'd have to bring along a sacrifice—I mean, distraction." Bryce's gray eyes were guileless.

Savannah was helpless to do anything other than laugh. "Who am I to say no to such a charming man's scheme?"

"I was hoping you'd say that. I even made sure I was in my spiffiest get-up just to impress you." He stood to his full height, which was quite impressive, being well over six foot, his stomach sucked in and his chest puffed out.

She made a show of looking him over slowly. What began as a tease soon turned serious as she appreciated just how fine a man he was. With his height, pewter gray eyes and square jaw, she could see why he had regularly made the most eligible bachelor list. She was somewhat amused to see that his face had slowly turned red as he held his breath in.

"I guess it'll do."

He let his breath out in a great gush. "Thank goodness for that. I'm not sure I would have been able to hold it for any longer." This was the Bryce she liked. The one that felt good just being around, that somehow made her better as a person because of his belief in her, the one quick to laugh. Her happy glow retreated under the dark cloud as memory of their date pushed its way to the surface. Bryce's face grew serious as he gazed at her, aware the mood had somehow shifted. "Should I worry about what thoughts make the light leave your eyes?"

His perceptive words jolted her. Her gaze flicked away guiltily. "Um, I was just thinking about when we went out for dinner."

Bryce looked, shamefaced, back at her, never breaking eye contact once he'd captured hers again. "Let's make a deal. This next one, that is the one we will call our first proper date, and we'll pretend like the last one never happened." Although his words were light—playful, even—there was a pleading in his eyes.

"I think I'd like that."

"Good. What are you doing tomorrow night?"

Savannah laughed, relaxing when she saw the tension ease around his eyes. "I'm at another rodeo."

"Hmm, well that won't do. When are you back home?"

"In a week."

"Good. I'll even be patient and give you a day to recover before we go on our date. I want it to be memorable."

Savannah stared at his earnest expression and smiled her agreeance. *I don't know. Last time was pretty memorable for me.*

CHAPTER 9

Savannah had been in the cozy confines of her trailer for so long that her bed at home felt too open and exposed. She'd spent a restless night trying to will herself to sleep and not think about her date the next day. Consequently, she was now lying in bed feeling like she had sandpaper for eyelids.

"Are you going to get out of bed or not, lazybones?" Savannah's eyes flew open at her sister's voice. She bolted upright, her feet not even touching the floor as she ran to embrace her twin.

"Oh my goodness, Ash! What on earth are you doing here?"

"Well, Kirk is off on some promotional tour for the week and I thought I might head home and see how my favorite sister was doing."

"I'm your only sister," Savannah reminded her.

"Well, all I can say is it's a good thing you didn't have any competition. Now brush your hair, I've made you a coffee." Savannah watched her smartly dressed sister saunter off into the kitchen. Only her sister would come home for a visit and wear designer clothes.

"Are you here for the whole week?" she called as she brushed her hair.

"Yep. I spent a couple of days with Mom and Dad, but you know how they get. Now I'm all yours. Well, I want to see the other girls as well." Ash handed her a steaming mug of coffee. She peered at her sister critically. "Rough night?"

"Just took me a while to settle into being back home I guess." Savannah didn't want to admit to her sister that she'd been nervous, let alone tell her about her date. But fate had other plans as her phone began to ring. A quick glance showed Bryce's name.

"Are you going to get that?"

"Get what?" Savannah decided to try and brazen it out.

Ash rolled her eyes in disgust at her obvious attempt at denial and pointed at the ringing device in her hand. "That phone. The one that's ringing." A sly look settled over her features, sending a spike of dread through Savannah. "Unless it's someone you don't want to answer in front of me. If it was someone you didn't want to talk to, you would just say 'oh, it's so and so, wish they'd stop calling me', but you didn't. So it must be that you aren't answering it because I'm here."

Ash leapt forward, forcing Savannah to take a defensive step sideways, splashing coffee. "Don't even think about it."

"Tell me who it is." Ash grappled to get her hands on the phone. "Or answer it, I don't care. Otherwise I'm going to answer it for you."

"Fine, I'll answer it. Happy?" Savannah brought the phone to her ear. "Hi, Bryce." She tried to ignore her sister's stunned face, her mouth forming a perfect 'O' before recovering and making kissing faces. Savannah rolled her eyes at her before turning her back to ignore her twin.

"Hi, sweetheart. How did you sleep last night? Glad to be back in your own bed?"

"Um, yeah. I think I've spent so long on the road that I would've slept better if I'd just gone out to the trailer to sleep."

Bryce laughed, sending a warmth through Savannah. "Are we still on for tonight?"

Savannah swatted Ash away as she tried to get her ear close enough to the phone to listen. "Yeah, I'm looking forward to it."

"Good, I'll be around to pick you up at seven, if that's all right with you?"

"Sure thing. I'll see you then." Savannah hung up the phone and glared at her sister. "That's not cool, and I have another thing I've been meaning to discuss with you. Did you tell Dad I liked Bryce?"

Ash giggled. "Yeah, but that was when you were just following him around like a little puppy. Wait until I tell him you're going on a date with him."

"Don't say anything."

"What happens if he asks me? It's Dad. I'm not going to lie to him."

"Oh my gosh, I'm never going to tell you anything again."

"You didn't have to tell me, it's pretty obvious. Anyway, you don't mean it. You always say that."

"This time, I do mean it." Savannah folded her arms determinedly.

Ash raised her brows doubtfully, clearly not believing her for a minute. "Okay. So, where's he taking you for dinner?"

Savannah slapped her forehead. "I forgot to ask."

"Rookie. How do you know what you're going to wear if you don't know where you're going?"

Savannah smiled smugly. "It doesn't matter where we're

going. I have the perfect outfit and, since you're here, you can make yourself useful and help with my hair."

"Sure. And then tomorrow you can tell me all about your date with Mr Bryce-the-most-eligible-cowboy-bachelor-five-years-running Dougson"

It was good to have Ash home.

THE HOURS ASH and Savannah had spent getting ready was worth it for the way Bryce's eyes grew gratifyingly wide at the sight of her. Forgotten in his hand was a huge bouquet of the biggest roses Savannah had ever seen. Each pale blush-colored bloom was the size of a softball. It was enough to set a girl's heart aflutter.

"I'm glad you picked that outfit to wear." His voice was gravelly, like a man dying from thirst.

"It's such a beautiful dress it seemed a shame not to wear it." Savannah's hands stole to her hips, smoothing down the white lace of her dress. As soon as Bryce had asked her to dinner, she'd known that she would pick the outfit he'd given her back when she'd been Ash's double for Frankie and Luciano's movie. She was hoping some of the magic that had made Luciano fall in love with Frankie would rub off.

"Hello, Bryce." Ash sauntered into the room, too impatient to remain in the kitchen. "Would you like me to take those flowers and put them in a vase of water?"

"Would you mind, Ash?" Savannah took them from Bryce, unable to resist inhaling their heady fragrance before handing them over. "They're beautiful."

"It's called the Juliet Rose and was a passion for its creator. It took him fifteen years to develop it." He smiled, the corners of his eyes crinkling. "I can understand how passion can override all common sense."

"Well, that's my cue to say goodnight," Ash said.

"And our cue to get going." Bryce held his hand out to Savannah. "Shall we?"

His hand felt warm as she slipped her much smaller hand into his. "We shall." Bryce retained his hold on her hand as he escorted her to his car and safely settled her into the passenger seat.

"Bryce, you were right."

"I'm not going to argue when a woman tells me that, but I might need a little more information."

"The doors are pretty cool."

He gunned the engine. "You wait till you feel how it goes." He looked boyish as he grinned at her eagerly.

She couldn't help but grin at him in return. "You haven't mentioned where we're going tonight," Savannah asked, suddenly curious.

"My place."

Savannah choked a little at his bluntness. "That's a little forward, don't you think?"

A smile ghosted his lips. "Just wait. I'm sure it will live up to my—and hopefully your—expectations."

Savannah mulled that over for the drive into the city as Bryce made small talk. From the underground parking, it surprised her when they took a private elevator directly up to his penthouse. When the doors opened, a wondrous sight greeted her eyes. Candles and flowers were everywhere. It looked like the love child of a florist and candlemaker. In the center of the room, a luxuriously appointed table stood pride of place and elegantly attired waitstaff stood to attention. At the head, was a man who looked like a butler Savannah had seen in a movie.

It was only when Bryce put some light pressure on the small of her back that she became aware she'd frozen in place. Yielding to his guiding hand, she entered the room, tantalizing aromas wafting from the kitchen.

"Bryce this is unlike anything I've ever seen," she said in awe.

"Thank you. I always try to exceed expectations." His expression was modest. "This is Bob, my butler," he said, introducing her to the man at the head of the table.

"Well, you certainly succeeded. Hello, Bob." Savannah did her level best to not look intimidated by the austere looking gentleman. "You have a butler and his name's Bob?"

"Of course. Bob makes my life so much easier." The efficient Bob spread the napkin over her lap and, with a flourish, poured some wine into one of several glasses on the table. Savannah was thankful as she hadn't been sure what they were all for.

"Tonight, we will be serving a degustation menu. The first course is paired with this sangiovese from the Napier Valley. I think you will find that it will bring out the flavors of your meal perfectly."

Savannah nodded, hoping she seemed like she knew what he'd said and waited for him to leave. Bob looked toward Bryce and, receiving a nod and gesture to leave the bottle, he haughtily stalked away.

"Bryce what's a disgusting course?"

He choked a little on the wine before valiantly draining the glass. "A degustation menu," he explained as he helped himself to more wine, "is when different wines are matched to courses to better bring out the flavors. Usually, each course is a small sample, so they usually have multiple courses. In this case, twelve."

Savannah could feel her mouth drop open. "I don't think I can eat twelve courses and still fit in this dress."

The look he gave her over the table was pure male

suggestion. "Well, I'm sure we can think of something to remedy the situation."

Savannah felt her face burn as she tried to brazen it out. She decided a change of subject was in order. "I've been meaning to talk to you—well, get some advice really. I have a few ideas for some clothing designs and, well, I'm thinking I might like to try designing some pieces."

Bryce sipped his wine. "I think that's a good idea. Maybe we could look at doing a limited-edition Savannah Decker collection and then, if there's interest, expand it out to a regular range."

Savannah hadn't known till he'd given it just how much his approval meant to her. She took in the sweeping vista of the cityscape to collect herself. When she turned back, it was to the first course being set in front of her and Bryce pouring another glass. And such set the scene for what was to be repeated another eleven times that evening.

At last, with a groan, she pushed away the empty dessert plate which was efficiently collected. She suspected the wait-staff were eager to be heading home. As if reading her thoughts, Bryce graciously waved one over and discreetly handed over what looked to be a substantial tip. With a look of gratitude and a few murmured words to his colleagues, Savannah found herself alone with Bryce.

Grabbing her wine glass, she stood and made her way over to the view that had captivated her all evening. She could hear Bryce's slightly uneven steps as he made his way over to join her. It disappointed her that he had continued to drink heavily throughout their meal.

"No matter how often I see it, I never get used to the beauty." The wisps of hair at the back of her neck fluttered gently with the breath of each word he spoke, so intimately close to her.

"It's an amazing view. I don't think I've ever been this high up to appreciate it."

"I was talking about you. No matter how often I see you, I never get used to how beautiful you are."

Vulnerable to his words, she turned to face him. His gaze when she met it was like a warm caress. Her eyes were drawn to his perfectly formed, full lips. That smile of his turned almost dangerously sexy. Savannah thought she would die of anticipation as he slowly lowered his head and pulled her into him, those luscious lips finally claiming her own.

And then, with a head-spinning swiftness, he released her. "Run as far away from me as possible."

Savannah blinked at the rapidness of being pulled from ecstasy to stunned confusion. "I don't understand," she stammered.

"I've never done anything but hurt the ones I love." There was an intensity to him that sent shivers of fear through her.

"Bryce, I know you could never hurt me." She reached out, letting her hand drop when he jerked away from her touch.

"Get away from me!" he yelled. Savannah's body jerked with fright, and he raised anguished eyes to her. "Don't you understand? I love you, and all I'll ever bring you is pain." When she still remained motionless, he stalked to the door, pausing to send the gorgeous tableware that had graced the table crashing to the ground. "I said leave!" he roared.

Before the last piece had completed its path to destruction, Savannah bolted from the room, running as fast as she could to escape his self-loathing torment.

CHAPTER 10

Bryce felt as though, sometime while he was asleep, a small rodent had crawled into his mouth and died. For some unknown reason, it appeared he'd chosen to sleep on the floor. He winced as he sat up, pulling shards of crockery from his shirt which he'd obviously ignored when he'd laid down. The room looked like it had been the host to a party of monkeys. He painfully squinted as he looked about, trying to take stock of what happened the previous evening. Horror stabbed at his already wretched brain as he recalled glimpses of the previous night and his abominable behavior to Savannah.

Why did he insist on this perverse torment? The more he wanted to pull Savannah close, the more he insisted on driving her away. The drink that had once brought him such welcome relief now served only to torture. A cold sweat broke out on his forehead. Once, it had helped drive the demons away. Now he feared it helped give them control.

OUTSIDE HER BEDROOM, Savannah could hear her sister moving around none too stealthily as she made herself some breakfast. She pulled the covers over her head. *Five, four, three, two, one.*

The impact of Ash's weight hitting her mattress almost launched Savannah from the bed. "I thought I heard you starting to get up. So how was it?"

Savannah freed herself from the cover that, moments before, had been a sanctuary but now held her tight like a prison. "I wasn't getting up. I was just lying here."

"Well, you were awake." Ash speared her with a steely look. "Now spill." Savannah pushed her matted hair from her face, not even sure where to begin. "When you get married, can I be your maid of honor? I'd add some Hollywood glamor."

"I don't think that's going to happen anytime soon."

"When Kirk and I get married, you know you'd be mine. I mean, you're my sister, after all."

"Hang on, so you'd only pick me cause I'm your sister? That hurts."

Ash scowled at her. "Well at least you would be mine. You don't even want me as yours."

"I'm not even getting married. Heck, I don't even know if I'll ever go on another date with Bryce Dougson again."

Ash dropped the teasing, her expression intrigued. "Seriously, what happened last night?"

"You need to promise you won't tell anyone. That includes but is not limited to Kirk, Dad, Teeny, Chloe, Mom, the girls, Suzie, and anyone else you might get the overwhelming urge to confide in."

"I promise." She held out her little finger. "Pinky swear?"

Savannah took it with her own. "Pinky swear."

Ash's expression ranged from curious, to amazed, to horrified, and ended in sympathy as Savannah's tale unfolded. She pressed her hand to her mouth. "Savannah, I don't know what to say. I never suspected he would act like that, he's always such a..." She waved her hands in the air, searching for the right description.

"Gentleman," Savannah finished for her.

"Yeah. Do you think he'll get help for his drinking problem?"

"I don't know. But I do know that, as much as I like him, I won't put up with the drunken mood swings and never being able to hang out without him drinking."

It saddened Savannah to say it, especially knowing how wounded Bryce was. But she knew enough to know that no one would be able to help Bryce if he didn't want to help himself. It said a lot about his strength of character that he'd been able to hide his problem for so long.

"Yeah, it's a pretty messed up situation for everyone. Come on, I need to top up my coffee and you look like you definitely need one."

Savannah trailed behind Ash out into the kitchen, grateful that her twin had been there when she'd needed her, even if she was a pain most of the time. She smiled, and Ash looked at her suspiciously.

"What's that for?"

"Nothing, but gosh, I've missed you."

"I'll deny it till my last breath if you ever tell anyone, but I've missed you, too." A knock interrupted her.

"Hold that thought," Savannah said, going to answer it. The moment the door swung open to reveal Bryce, she remembered, to her horror, that she was still dressed in her old baggy pajamas, her hair matted into a bird's nest and her teeth in desperate need of brushing.

Bryce stood awkwardly on the threshold, sunglasses in place, hat in hand, and flowers at his side. "May I please come in?"

Savannah pursed her lips. He wasn't her most favorite person in the world after last night, but she still liked the guy. "Okay."

He held the obviously very expensive orchids out to her and, after she accepted them, he removed his sunglasses to expose bloodshot painful eyes, a look that she was becoming only too familiar with. Savannah had a flashback to when he'd last been there under very similar circumstances.

"Look, I have no excuse for last night."

Savannah felt her brow arch. "So you remember it?"

He winced at her caustic tone. "More than I'd like to admit. I'm sorry. I should never have let that happen."

She looked down at the delicate orchids, biting her lip. "You scared me last night."

"I scared me last night, too. I've always been able to handle my drinking, but lately, it's gotten a lot worse. I used to be able to control it and now it controls me." Bryce's gaze slid away, embarrassed at admitting his weakness.

"Is it that you don't like being around me? Am I the problem?" Savannah felt sick to the pit of her stomach even asking the question, but she had to know.

His gaze rocketed back to hers and he took a step forward, gently cupping her chin, making it impossible for her to drop her eyes. "No, this is all my fault. I've made an appointment with an alcohol counselor to help me conquer it once and for all. I think I drank to help me not feel after Lily, and then, being around you, all I do is feel. I've never been so scared in my life as when I'm with you."

Savannah looked down at her much smaller stature and back up to his much larger one. "You're scared of me?" Her face scrunched up in disbelief.

"I'm broken, Savannah." The pain in his words made Savannah's heart constrict. "And you're so vibrant and full of life. I feel like a moth drawn to the flames when I'm near you, but I'm so scared I'll pull your wings off and I won't even mean to."

Savannah gently stroked Bryce's cheek, the stubble rough beneath her palm. "I'm strong. The only thing that will break me is if you don't get your drinking under control."

Bryce took her hand and gently kissed her palm. "I won't ever put you in that situation again."

"Good. Because if you ever act like that again, no amount of apologies and expensive flowers will make it better."

CHAPTER 11

The highway lines shone iridescently white in Savannah's truck's high beams. Above, the stars twinkled merrily beside the glowing white of the moon, each crater clear. Nova had placed again that night, but this time, there'd been no time to stop and celebrate. They'd started to gain momentum and, no sooner had she finished her run, then it was time to load up, drive all night, and repeat at the next one.

Savannah was grateful that Miranda was still with her. Her friend had been apologetic when she'd called to ask if she could do the next run of rodeos with her, her own rig still not fixed. Secretly, Savannah had been relieved. Somehow, it felt like they were a little team on the road together. Sometimes it almost felt like she'd figured out this rodeo gig and wasn't just surviving but was thriving. She reached for her can of energy drink. Nothing was going to stop her now. She was determined to be the champion she'd always dreamed of.

Miranda shifted in her seat, trying to find a more

comfortable position. "Hey, do you want me to drive for a while?" she asked groggily.

"I'm good for a bit longer. I'm still amped after tonight's win."

"How many is that in a row now?"

"Eight in a row for wins, fifteen in a row for placing."

Miranda pulled her hoodie up, preparing to go back to sleep. "Well, if anyone deserves it, it's you. Wake me up if you want me to drive."

"Sure thing." Savannah smiled as the white lines continued to flash by in a seemingly never-ending rhythm. Life was good.

"HEY, Miranda, have you seen my watch?" Savannah pulled the cushions back from the pull-out sofa, looking to see if it might have fallen down. "I swear I left it on the kitchenette bench."

Miranda walked in from her bedroom, brushing her hair. "No, I haven't seen it." She stopped brushing to stare at Savannah in concern. "I'm starting to get scared with all this stuff that keeps going missing. I mean, it's only been small stuff up till now, but your watch? You hardly ever take that off." Her eyes grew wide and she looked around as if expecting to find someone in the trailer. "Do you think someone is watching us?"

A shiver of terror ran up Savannah's spine, goosebumps erupting on her arms. "Don't say something like that. I'm not going to be able to sleep now."

"I'm getting really freaked out, Savannah."

"Me too. I'm going to call Bryce." It said a lot for how used to things going missing she was starting to get that she was pleasantly surprised to find her phone where she'd left it. She quickly punched in his number.

"Hey, sweetheart. I was just about to call you."

"Bryce, Miranda and I are starting to feel scared."

"What happened?" There was a deadly intensity to his voice, relief washing over Savannah that he was taking her seriously.

"For about a week, little things have been going missing. And I mean, it started off with silly things, like hair ties, or toothpaste. Then, this morning, we came back from watering the horses and there was a packet of chewing gum on the kitchenette bench and it's not a flavor that either Miranda or I like and now I can't find my watch. It's one that Mom and Dad bought for me and Ash when we graduated from high school. It's a matching set."

"Okay, Savannah, this is what we're going to do. First, I want you to go to Miranda and you gals stay together. I'm going to call Colt—I think he's at the same rodeo. Keep the door locked until he gets there, okay? I'm going to get there as soon as I can, but that may not be till morning."

Savannah's heart was thumping uncomfortably in her chest. "I'm going to find her now, she's just in the other room."

"Good girl. I'm going to stay on the phone with you till you do and then I'm gonna call Colt and call you straight back and stay on the line till he gets there."

Miranda looked petrified sitting on the sofa when she opened the door. Savannah hurried to her and the girls huddled together for what felt like an eternity till Colt called out to say he was outside. She'd never been so happy to see someone before in her life. He tipped his hat to her. "I hear y'all have a bit of an unwanted guest."

Now that Colt was there, she was beginning to feel a bit

ridiculous. "We don't know for sure, but there's been some strange things going on."

"I'll have a bit of a look around out here and then a mosey inside, if you'd like."

"That'd be great." Bryce called back just as Colt disappeared around the side of the trailer with his flashlight.

"Are you okay? I've been trying to reach you, but it kept saying the call failed."

"I don't know what happened. I've had my phone with me the whole time. Colt's here now. He's just going to look around outside and then check inside. I feel a bit silly now."

"Sweetheart, always—and I mean always—trust your gut instinct. I'd rather it all be for nothing than have something happen to you." Savannah felt a warm glow at his obvious concern. "If it's all right with you, I've asked Colt to bunk down with you gals tonight. He can sleep on the sofa, but it should give you peace of mind and hopefully some sleep."

"That would be good, as long as he doesn't mind."

"He doesn't. And I'll be there as soon as I can."

"I'm sorry to be such a pain." Although it did feel quite nice to have Bryce protecting her, even if it was remotely.

"You aren't. I don't want anything happening to my gal." *His gal.*

"Colt's on his way back now, so I'd better go. Thank you, Bryce, I already feel a lot safer."

"Goodnight, sweetheart. I'll be there to keep you safe myself tomorrow."

Once Colt had been safely ensconced on the sofa with a pillow and spare blanket, it surprised Savannah how quickly her eyelids grew heavy. The last thought that flitted across her sleepy mind was *my gal.* She was Bryce's gal.

~

BRYCE HUNG UP THE PHONE. From the corner of the room, he looked at the empty space where his bourbon used to sit. He needed something to calm down the beating of his heart and the tremor in his hands. When Savannah had called, it had been all he could do not to jump straight into his private plane and go after her. Sure, he'd known that his pilot wouldn't be ready for hours and the earliest he'd be able to make it was morning, but his primal instincts had kicked in. His woman was in danger, darn it, and he needed to protect her.

He was grateful Colt was there to keep watch over her. He owed that guy big time. As a guy of action, it was hard to now sit calmly and wait. He glanced down at his watch. Somewhere, a bar would be open. His hands reached for his keys before he even processed the thought further, his mouth craving the sweet bourbon taste and his mind the blessed numbness it brought. And then a pair of emerald green eyes stared at him in disappointment, his mind conjuring up the one thing he loved more than the drink. Bryce stood in silent battle, his love for Savannah warring with the addiction his body demanded. Finally, he forced his hand to release the keys and, with a muttered curse, headed to the shower. It was going to be a long night.

IT HAD BEEN two weeks since Bryce had joined the girls on the road, and it had been interesting to say the least. Miranda seemed to resent having him around, always eager to pick on something he'd done, but would then mention how nice it was not to feel scared all the time. Bryce, for his part, had so far managed to resist rising to her baiting, all the while trying to run his business remotely. It made Savannah love him even more that he was willing to not only to drop everything he'd been doing to come when she'd needed him, but also tolerate her friend and do all of that sober.

One thing no one could argue with was that things had mysteriously stopped going missing. Sadly, none of the lost items had been recovered either, and Savannah felt the loss of her watch in particular.

"I thought I might find you here." Bryce sat down at the back of the trailer where she'd been cleaning her gear.

"You were busy on the Zoom meeting and I didn't want to interrupt. Miranda is off checking out the grounds somewhere I think."

"I'm not going to complain that I have you all to myself." A couple of cowboys walked by, one cracking open a can of beer, the foam erupting, causing his friends to laugh. Bryce watched keenly, his hands beginning to shake.

"I know it's not easy, being here with alcohol pretty much everywhere. It mustn't be easy to have temptation right under your nose all the time." Savannah gave his hand a squeeze. "I'm proud of you."

"Yeah, well, I do miss bourbon, I can tell you. But I'd miss you more." Bryce leaned over and gave her a kiss.

Savannah placed her hand over her heart. "Well, that's enough to turn a girl's head."

"Well, if that doesn't work, I hope this will." He handed her a small bottle green box.

She looked at him in surprise. "What's this?"

"I think you will discover that, if you open it, you'll find out." Savannah poked out her tongue as she complied. Inside was a stunning platinum and diamond Rolex watch. Her eyes huge, she stared up at him, speechless. "I'm sorry I couldn't get the exact watch you lost. I even had Ash take a picture of hers, but they don't make them anymore."

"Bryce, you are the only man I know that gives a woman a Rolex and apologizes for it. It's beautiful." She took his face in her hands and kissed him soundly. Her heart sung at this wondrously flawed man she was lucky enough to call hers.

"I take it you like it then?" He laughed.

"I love it. Bryce, I don't know how I can thank you for taking time out of your busy schedule when I needed you. I know it has been a lot of extra stress for you to be here and you haven't complained once. I just want you to know it means a lot to me." Savannah blinked, her emotions overcoming her.

Gently, he stroked her jawline with his thumb, his soulful eyes piercing her soul. "I will always be here when you need me. Nothing is more important to me than you. Savannah, I believe in you, I want you to chase your dreams with everything you have as far as they will take you. Somehow, I got lucky, and I'm the guy that gets to go on this adventure with you. I've done some things in my life I'm not proud of and I know I don't deserve any of this, but I will never be happier than when I'm with you."

Savannah knew she was about to make her ugly crying face. "I'm happiest with you, too." She sniffled.

"I will never understand how women can be happy and crying at the same time."

"You don't have to understand. All you have to do is come here and kiss me."

"I think I can do that." He pulled her in close, his gorgeous gray eyes staring intently into hers before lowering his head and, at last, doing exactly what he was told.

CHAPTER 12

It felt like Bryce had been part of their dysfunctional trio for a lifetime. A sorrowful ripple of melancholy made Savannah sigh. The very thought of him leaving that day made her glum but she had no right to complain. After all, the man had delayed the inevitable for as long as possible and he really needed to get back to his work commitments. To be fair to the man, there were only so many business meetings he could hold from the bedroom of her trailer. She smiled apologetically as she opened the door to retrieve a hat—Bryce had been holed up in there for a while talking on the phone to Silvia.

"I want to see a proposal from them before I promise any money. I want to know exactly where they are allocating their budget spend." Bryce listened intently to what Silvia said. "I agree, I'm happy with the others. Just to confirm, that's one million to the Cancer Foundation, one million to the Starlight Foundation and another million to Doctors Without Borders. I'll look through the rest of the proposals when I get back."

Savannah quietly closed the door behind her, feeling

teary at Bryce's generosity. She'd always known he had a kind heart and his charity work reinforced that. She turned the kettle on and waited for it to boil. A nice cup of coffee and a bit of a relax on the sofa seemed heavenly. She was surprised when Bryce walked out of the bedroom and then out of the trailer without saying a word. *What on earth?*

A moment later, he returned, his hands held awkwardly behind his back. "What the heck are you doing?" She could feel a silly smile stretch her lips at the comical sight. Whatever it was, judging from the way Bryce was trying to keep a grip on it, was very wiggly.

"I have to leave and I really don't want to. But as good as Colt is at helping when I can't be here, I think this fella will do a much better job at it." He pulled a squirming, licky German shepherd pup from behind his back and, with aplomb, handed it over to her eager, outstretched arms.

"Oh, Bryce." Savannah giggled as the pup licked her face. "He's about the cutest thing I've ever seen."

"Well, he's also a very tough and scary guard dog."

She giggled again as the pup tried his best to snuggle under her arm, giving her his most appealing puppy face, all floppy ears trying to stand up and wiggling, fuzzy body. "I'm sure he is. He'll also make the cutest hot water bottle to cuddle up with in bed when I'm feeling lonely."

As soon as she said the words, she felt bad. All the happiness disappeared from Bryce's face to be replaced with guilt. "I wish I didn't have to go. I can try putting it off for another week."

She pulled him in close, no mean feat with the puppy still taking up prime real estate on her lap. "Don't you dare. I'm a big girl, and nothing funny has happened for weeks now. I love what you did for me, coming here and being my knight in shining armor. I know I'm important to you. You make me feel that way every day, even when you're not here. I'm not going to break when you need to focus on other aspects of your life."

It felt like the roles had suddenly been reversed, his face lighting up as the tension that had been shadowing it lifted. For some odd reason, Savannah felt like she'd just given him a gift. He wrapped his arms around her, the puppy squirming, trying to lick both of their faces. "Have you decided what you're going to call him?"

She looked down at the fuzzy furball that was now trying to eat the button off her shirt. "Well he looks like trouble. How about Harry?"

Bryce tilted his head as he looked critically at the pup. "I think you're right about the trouble. All right, Harry the handful it is."

Savannah gave him a kiss. "Thank you."

"Somehow, I think I'm going to spend the rest of my life trying to get you to smile and look at me like that." He gave her another kiss and Savannah thought her heart would explode with love for him. This man was more than she'd ever imagined. "I really don't want to go, but if I don't leave now, I'm going to miss my flight."

Savannah was reluctant to let him leave her embrace. "Don't you have a private plane?"

"Yes, but even private planes have to adhere to flight plans they submit. And if I don't go now, I don't think I'll be able to make myself leave you." He stopped his slow backing away to stare deeply into her eyes, his own swirling with emotions. He swallowed thickly, as if the words were lodged in his throat.

"You don't have to say it. I know."

In an instant, he moved toward her and wrapped his arms around her, pulling her close. She closed her eyes and breathed in his scent, and then he was gone, leaving her and Harry alone. Savannah snuggled the puppy, doing her best not to get his fur wet with her tears. Now that he was gone, she could cry. She knew it was silly. He would call her every day, probably several times a day, and she'd see him soon. But somehow, this time together had connected them and bonded them tightly in a way she'd never expected. She loved him, and now this separation from him caused her heart anguish. Savannah cradled Harry and let the tears continue to flow. She would wallow in her misery for a little longer, time soon enough to put her big girl pants on.

SAVANNAH WASN'T sure how long she remained curled up with the puppy. When she finally emerged from her self-pity, a quick look around found that Bryce had left a bag filled with dog food, treats, toys, a bed and basically everything a spoilt Harry would need near the door. She smiled. It was Bryce summed up in one thoughtful gesture.

"Hey, when did we get a dog?" Miranda asked as she stepped into the trailer.

"We just did. Bryce got him for me." Savannah proudly held the pup out. "Let me introduce you to Harry, protector of cowgirls and giver of kisses and snuggles."

Miranda scooped him up in her arms and rubbed her cheek against his soft fur. "Wow, if Bryce leaves us a puppy every time he goes, he can come back anytime he wants."

Savannah felt a twinge of sadness at her friend's words. *Big girl pants*, she reminded herself. "Yeah, it was nice to have him around."

Miranda giggled as Harry licked her chin. "Well, aren't you the cutest thing." She looked up at Savannah. "I meant to tell you, I got word this morning that they've finally finished fixing my truck and I've even managed to save enough money to pay for it."

A wave of sadness washed over Savannah. Now Miranda was leaving her, too! "It's okay if you want to keep traveling together. It's nice having the company, and there's a cute puppy to throw into the deal now."

Miranda kissed Harry on the head. "And he's a very cute puppy too. If it's all right, I'll stay with you for the next few events and then I'll go pick up my rig. I think I might take Ed to a few of the smaller events and get him running better away from the crowds. Maybe when I come back, I'll give you and Nova a run for your money."

Savannah tried to smile bravely. "At least I'll have Harry for company." The puppy, seeming to recognize his name, wiggled to free himself from Miranda's hold. Her friend set him gently on his feet and he ran toward Savannah. She picked him up, enjoying the warmth of his body. "What more could I ask for?"

CHAPTER 13

The time flew by and, before Savannah knew it, it was the last night Miranda would be her traveling companion. She had, by now, had time to get herself used to the idea that she would be on the road by herself and strangely, now that she'd had time for it to sink in, she was looking forward to being a tough cowgirl on the road with nothing but her horse and dog.

"You know, we need to have a drink," Savannah commented as they both unsaddled their horses after their rounds. "It's going to be ages till I see you again."

"I know. But as soon as I get this big lug"—Miranda affectionately looked at her horse—"as soon as he comes into some sort of form, I'm hitting the big rodeos again. We need to make sure we always park side by side so we can be neighbors and I can hang out in yours, cause it's a lot flasher than mine."

"Hey, promise me you'll come to Frankie and Luciano's grand opening of their training ranch. You need to see the facilities. It will blow your mind."

"Try and stop me."

Savannah looked down at her beeping phone and quickly read the message, a giddy smile bursting from her. "No way."

Her friend's brows were drawn together in confusion. "No way what?"

"Gabi had her baby. It's a little girl." Happiness suffused her. She couldn't wait to meet the newest Affinity Ranch baby.

"Wow, that's awesome. What's her name?"

"Maria Ana Rojas." She looked at her friend when the significance hit her, and she became emotional. "They named her after both of their mothers." She held her hand to her heart. "Isn't that just the sweetest thing ever?"

"It's adorable. Well, it looks like we really will need to go get that drink. We can't not celebrate the baby."

"Just let me quickly send a text and I'll be ready to go." Savannah rapidly fired off a message to Bryce, suddenly feeling like part of a very grownup couple discussing friends' babies.

Miranda waited impatiently, tapping her foot. "I'm getting thirsty."

Savannah was just about to slip the phone back into her pocket when Bryce's reply came through, suggesting that they get a gift together. She quickly agreed, smiling happily to herself. Maybe Bryce was feeling like a couple, too. "Okay, all done."

"Finally." Miranda dramatically began to cough. "I thought I was about to perish from thirst."

"Well, I'm waiting for you."

Miranda began to splutter indignantly, and Savannah solicitously patted her on the back. "There, there. Now, when you're ready, I'd really like to get a drink." And with one final thump, she walked off in the direction of the bar, whistling merrily to herself.

SAVANNAH WOKE FEELING a little worse for wear. She lay in bed for a moment getting her orientation before deciding she really needed to get a glass of water. She looked down at her watch and was surprised to see it was mid-morning. She was eternally grateful that this was a two-day rodeo and she'd made it through to the short round and didn't have to drive anywhere today. Closing the refrigerator door, she spied a note on the kitchenette bench. Picking it up, she read it.

Savannah,

You were sleeping so soundly I didn't want to wake you. I'm going to get my truck and then I'll be back this evening to get Ed. I know you will be spectacular tonight.

Miranda

PS I've fed Nova and Harry for you.

Savannah looked down to where Harry was sniffing around his empty food bowl, giving her the puppy dog eyes that swore he hadn't been fed. "Don't even try it." She waved the note at him. "I know better." Still feeling a little worse for wear, she grabbed his leash. Maybe a bit of fresh air was just what the doctor ordered, and she really didn't want to take any chances with Harry having a toilet accident in the trailer. She didn't think her stomach would be able to handle it.

Much later, after quiet time laying on the sofa in her trailer, Savannah finally felt almost human again. *Darn girl, what on earth was in those drinks last night?* To the best of her knowledge, she could only remember having had three beers, and that was over a couple of hours.

She admired the way the little diamonds on her watch caught the light and sparkled as she checked the time. "Better get up and start getting ready," she said to Harry, still sprawled out on the couch. A quick change and she was out the door, primed to saddle up Nova. When she went to

Nova's stall, the filly was restless, amped up. She stood on Savannah's toes several times and she paced, making it difficult to catch her.

"Darn it, Nova, stand still already," she said in frustration. After a few long minutes, she finally managed to halter her and lead her back to the trailer. There the battle continued and, by the time she had her saddled, Savannah was flustered, conscious that the buffer of time she liked to give herself had been eaten into.

She quickly tried to check her cinch and mount, Nova again making things difficult with sidestepping away from her and making Savannah hop after her. In frustration, she only gave it a cursory check. Once she was in the saddle, Savannah tried to breathe in deeply to release the tension in her body. Nova pranced underneath her, unwilling to stand quietly. Feeling her frustration rising and her filly coiled like a spring beneath her, she did her best to harness the power and headed toward the warmup. With only five minutes before her round, she could only pray that she could work the silliness out of her horse.

By the time she was called over, Savannah was beginning to have serious misgivings about taking Nova into the arena. The filly had always been quirky, but maybe Nova was being affected by the atmosphere. Savannah wasn't sure what else it could be, but she was bordering on being uncontrollable. "Quitters aren't champions, and champions aren't quitters," she muttered to herself. Giving a quick nod to the gate steward before she changed her mind, she managed to get Nova in, albeit almost taking the steward out with the filly's swinging hindquarters.

Knowing she didn't dare stop her once in the alley, she set her heels into the buckskin's side and sent her rocketing out onto the sand of the arena. It felt like she was strapped to a missile—and with as much control—over the course.

Coming into the first barrel, Nova completely ignored her when she tried to rate her speed, not taking a pull out at all, and only making it around the drum without mishap by the barest of margins.

As they charged to the second, Savannah decided she didn't care what people thought, she was aborting this run. Too late, she realized that Nova well and truly had the bit between her teeth and no amount of pulling on the reins was going to slow her down. Coming into the barrel, all Savannah could do was grab hold of the saddle horn and hope for the best. The ground was choppy, and she could feel the filly scrambling for traction. Something was very wrong. The saddle was no longer perfectly balanced. Instead, it lurched to one side and she was falling between Nova's legs and then, nothing but blackness.

"I think she's starting to come to." The room seemed too bright as Savannah opened her eyes, her head throbbing painfully.

"Careful, young lady," a strange man said kindly as she struggled to sit up. "How 'bout you just lay there a bit longer. You've had a nasty bump to your head."

Savannah complied, looking around the room she was in and realizing she was in the Black Angus Sports Medicine trailer. The door opened, and a worried looking Colt entered, relief making him smile when he saw that she was awake. "How you feeling?"

"Like I tried to stop my fall with my head." For the first time, she wondered where her horse was and if she was okay. "Where's Nova?"

"She's fine. I caught her and she's back in her stall. Is she like that often? I remember her being a lot calmer, but this time she was a real handful."

Savannah bristled at the criticism to her filly. "She's young and usually she's fine. I think maybe the atmosphere got to her or something." She closed her eyes, suddenly tired. "But she's okay?"

"She's fine, no sign of lameness," Colt assured her.

"Oh my gosh, Savannah! Are you okay?" Miranda rushed through the door, Harry in her arms. "I just got back and heard." Harry wiggled free and jumped up to get to Savannah. Colt picked him up and placed him on the bed.

"I'm fine. At least, I think I'm fine," Savannah said, looking at the man she assumed was a doctor for confirmation.

"She has a concussion, but she's very lucky it wasn't worse. She can't be left alone for a few days and I don't want her driving either," the doctor said.

"That's all right, I'll drive her home," promised Miranda.

"But you just picked up your truck," protested Savannah.

"I'll take Ed home now and then be back in time to drive you home tomorrow." Miranda looked at Colt. "Will you be able to stay with her for tonight and make sure nothing happens?"

"Sure thing."

"Miranda, that seems like a lot of bother. I'll call Chloe and see if she can come out and drive me back," Savannah said, uncomfortable at putting her friend out so much.

"Nonsense. It's all arranged. I'll leave you here in the doctor and Colt's capable hands and will see you in the morning." Without another word, Miranda bustled out of the room.

"You have a good friend there," the doctor commented.

"The best," agreed Savannah. "The very best."

CHAPTER 14

There was something to be said to having everyone fussing around. Some people didn't like it, but Savannah was firmly in the affirmative camp. After Miranda had driven her and Nova home, Chloe had made sure she was settled in bed and cooked a lovely breakfast for her before heading off to work. Sra Ana had turned up with a week's worth of food in containers and then Bryce had arrived with flowers and silk monogramed pajamas. He'd joked that, since she was going to be lounging around, he wanted to make sure she was suitably attired. All in all, now that the shock of what had happened had worn off, it was a pretty sweet deal.

Now she impatiently waited while the doctor checked her reactions to make sure she didn't have any lingering effects from her concussion. It was hard to tell if the doctors little "hmms" were good or bad. After one last test, he took his seat behind his desk. "I would say, Ms Decker, that you are very lucky, and it looks like you are in the clear. I would strongly suggest that you don't have any more head knocks in the next twelve months."

"Well, that's the plan." Savannah immediately regretted her trite answer upon receiving a very unamused look from the good doctor. "Um." She cleared her throat. "So I'm okay to drive, you know, now I have the all clear?"

"You are able to drive."

Savannah fairly skipped from the room and out to where Bryce had been patiently waiting. "Was the doc happy with your recovery?" he asked, wrapping an arm around her as they walked from the waiting room.

"Yep, I'm allowed to do everything again. So, if you don't want to be my chauffeur today, I'll understand."

Bryce's eyes went wide, his hand going to his chest at the affront. "I can't think of anything else I would rather do than drive you around. And I've already cleared my schedule for the day, so you're not getting rid of me that easily."

"Good, because I have some visiting I want to do."

Senhor Eduardo was on his usual blanket under the Live Oak tree. Savannah considered if maybe she should buy him a bigger one, or at least another one to put down with it, as he seemed to be running out of blanket real estate these days. Gracie was no longer ever-present now that she attended elementary school. Instead, she'd been replaced with a host of smaller companions for the silver-haired Brazilian grandfather. Edward, now a stocky little boy, ran away, all high-knee action and very little forward momentum, and giggled infectiously as only small children can, wanting to be chased. The dark-haired twins—the slightly bigger Luciano Jnr and his more delicate but feisty sister, Harper—crawled and tried to pull themselves up on whatever they could get their tiny grasping hands on. And there, in a pair of chairs that had been brought out, sat Sra Ana, besotted beside her daughter, Gabi, as she nursed her tiny infant.

Spying them, Sra Ana waved them over. "Come, come. You have not met my newest grandbaby, Maria Ana. Is she not beautiful?"

Savannah looked down into inky black, sleepy eyes, her face still squishy in the way only newborns were. To be honest, at the rate the Affinity Ranch ladies had been having babies, she was beginning to worry there might be something in the water. "She's gorgeous."

"Bryce, you need to have a hold. It will be good practice for when you have one of your own."

Bryce looked terrified. "Ma'am, I'm not sure that's a good idea. I don't want to be responsible for something happening to that little baby."

Savannah watched amused as Sra Ana skewered him with a look that brooked no argument. She stood and pointed to her now vacant chair. "Sit."

Like an obedient puppy, he sat. She rewarded him with a smile and she tenderly took her granddaughter from Gabi and placed him in Bryce's arms. Savannah wasn't even sure if he was breathing as he held the baby with infinite tenderness. He stared down at the blanket-wrapped bundle, a look of terror-stricken awe on his face. Slowly, he raised his eyes to meet hers. This wounded man of hers had so much love to give and, one day, he would make an amazing father. Of that she was sure.

Sra Ana nodded with approval, obviously happy with the care he was giving Maria Ana. "You will be staying for lunch." It was more of an order than a question.

"Yes, ma'am."

"Good, you can stay with Senhor Eduardo and mind the children. The women will get the food."

"Ma'am," he began.

"Sra Ana," she corrected.

He smiled at her like a schoolboy that had just been given the class prize. "Sra Ana, I'm more than happy to let Gabi enjoy her time out here with her baby, and Savannah really should be taking it easy. How about I help you in the kitchen?"

Sra Ana smiled slowly. "I would be happy to show you what I need done." Bryce very slowly stood and, ever so gently, transferred the now sleeping baby back to her mother. Gabi smiled at him before giving her daughter a tender kiss on the head. Bryce gave Savannah's hand a quick squeeze before he headed off with Sra Ana toward the house. Savannah gave an amused shake of her head as she watched the large cowboy amble off with the much smaller silver-haired Brazilian woman. Her big cowboy surrounded by children and babies and meekly following the orders of a grandma. What would his business competitors say if they could see him now?

"I DON'T KNOW if I can even think about having dinner after that lunch we had." Bryce patted his extended belly. "Does she always put on that much food? I just assumed whenever she catered an event that she cooked a lot, but now I'm beginning to think she's just a feeder."

Savannah laughed. "She once told me that food is love. So, she must love you a whole lot."

Bryce's expression turned serious and he left the room they had just walked into. Savannah stared awkwardly out the floor-to-ceiling windows of the penthouse, wondering what had just happened. Before she could invest much further energy into her speculations, he returned, holding a small blue box tied with a white ribbon. Startled, her eyes flew to his face. Was that what she thought it was?

Bryce, anticipating her unvoiced question, quickly held a hand up to stall her. "This isn't a ring. One day, I promise I'll give you one so big you won't be able to lift your hand. This is something that I wanted to give you to show you what you mean to me and, I guess, as a promise." He held the box out to her.

Savannah untied the ribbon and opened the box. Inside, on white satin, lay a single pink diamond pendant suspended on a white gold chain. The jewelry was simplicity itself in its design, the large stone extravagant enough that it needed no further embellishment. She stared up at him, her eyes shimmering. "Bryce, it's beautiful, but you really don't need to buy me things like this."

"I know, and I love that you don't expect me to buy these things for you. It just makes me want to do it more." He held his hand out for the necklace and, after a moment's hesitation, she complied. He took it and walked behind her, gently reaching over to put it around her neck. Savannah pulled her hair out of the way before her fingers shakily found a path to the pendant. It felt cool beneath her touch. "It's an Argyle Pink Diamond—three carats, to be precise—all the way from Australia. It's the largest mine in the world that has pink diamonds and it has almost come to the end of the deposit. When I saw it, I thought of you. Something rare and precious that doesn't need anything else to shine." Bryce stepped around to admire the jewel. "It's beautiful, just like you. I want you to wear it for luck, and know I'm with you, even when I can't be."

"Bryce, I don't know if I can wear this, it's too valuable." Savannah didn't even want to hazard a guess at the value of what she wore around her throat.

"A beautiful lady deserves beautiful things. Savannah, I

can afford to spoil you." He guided her to a mirror hung on the wall. Savannah looked at the diamond, a pink that she'd never seen before glinting in the light. Its color was so vivid that, as she turned it to capture the light, it almost seemed to have hints of purple.

"I want to argue with you, Bryce, but it's gorgeous." She turned and threw herself into his arms. "I love it, thank you."

"I meant what I said before. One day, it will be a ring that I give you." He lowered his head and kissed her. Savannah closed her eyes and savored the kiss, her heart singing with happiness.

CHAPTER 15

"Almost packed?" Frankie asked as Savannah hefted her saddle into place on the rack in the trailer.

"Yep, Nova hasn't put a foot wrong since we've been back. I'm at a loss to what happened, what triggered her going crazy like that." Savannah stepped down from the back of the trailer.

"It's a worry," Frankie agreed. "If you don't know what caused it, you don't know when it will happen again." Her face was serious, strained under the weight of her concern. "Savannah, if she even comes close to doing anything like that again … well—" Frankie sighed unhappily, her gaze darting away. "I know I promised she'd be your ride for as long as you wanted her. But if I decide she's too dangerous, I'm sorry, but you won't be a team anymore."

Savannah stared at her boss in surprise. Sure, she knew what happened with Nova had been dangerous. But she didn't feel it had been deliberate from the filly either. "Frankie," she began to protest.

Frankie held up her hand. "I don't want to talk anymore about it. I'm bloody sick to my stomach even thinking about what happens if there is a next time. All I can do is pray that it was a once-off and leave it at that." Savannah knew all about feeling sick to her stomach. Not trusting herself to speak, she nodded. "Now, after this trip, I need you to come straight home. They want me to do a presentation as part of the grand opening. Chloe and I are going to show some methods on how we train our horses, but I want you there, too. I was thinking maybe we could do a demonstration riding Sampson and Nova without any tack on. Well, at least that's what I thought before Nova went all crazy."

"I want to do it. You have to believe me when I say that, whatever happened, it won't happen again. I won't let it." Savannah smiled at her mentor. It meant a lot to her that Frankie thought she was good enough to do a demonstration with.

"Good. Well, just try to come back in one piece and we can brainstorm some ideas with what we are going to do for it."

Savannah watched Frankie walk away. She knew she had nothing but the best intentions at heart, but there was no way she was going to let anyone take Nova away from her. The only thing left to do was prove the buckskin could be trusted. Speaking of which, she grabbed the halter. Time to get her horse and hit the road. Whistling softly to herself, she headed out into the field to catch one filly that was sorely in need of redeeming herself.

HER SHOULDERS FELT STIFF AND, for what seemed like the hundredth time that evening, Savannah rolled them, trying to loosen the kinks. She took another long chug of her energy drink, turned the radio up louder, and wound her window down, hoping the cool air would help revive her.

She was still a good couple of hours away from the rodeo ground and, at that moment, every minute felt like it was crawling by. Maybe she'd gotten soft with having Miranda around to share the driving duties, but all she knew was she was feeling tired and wished she was there already.

A soft snore came from her passenger seat. Savannah glanced down to where Harry was curled up in a doggy bed, fast asleep. She smiled. Well, at least she wasn't alone.

Suddenly, bright lights lit up the interior of the cab, making it look like it was the middle of the day. Her brain struggled to make sense of it. A truck was blocking her lane, pulling out from a truck stop. Frantically, she hit the brakes, but she wasn't slowing down, her pedal dropping straight to the floor. In the split second before impact, she reached out to grab Harry and then, blessed nothing.

GROGGILY, she opened her eyes, fighting against the darkness that tried to pull her back down into its depth. The light seemed a little too bright, and harsh chemical smells made her crinkle her nose.

"Nice of you to join us in the land of the living." She turned her head painfully to see Bryce sitting beside her. With infinite care, he leaned forward and held her close. "I'm beginning to think you're making a habit out of this." His voice sounded raw, like he'd been crying.

Savannah looked blankly at him. "What do you mean?" Her throat felt scratchy, like she hadn't swallowed for a while, the words sounding hoarse from lack of use. Her body seemed oddly still.

"Getting hurt." He gestured around them. "Ending up in hospital."

"Why am I here?"

He stared at her oddly, leaning away to look her in the face intently, but not before capturing her hand that lay limply on the bed. "You don't remember?"

"No," Savannah realized now that her arm felt heavy because it was in a plaster cast. "What happened?"

"Sweetheart, you were in a car crash. You were headed to Wyoming for a rodeo and never made it."

"Is Nova okay? What about Harry?" Her heart began to pound wildly in her chest, what if something had happened to them? Why couldn't she remember? She tried to sit up. Something jabbed into her hand and she realized she was hooked up to an IV.

"Savannah, you need to calm down." Bryce's voice was soothing as he gently took hold of her shoulders. Savannah struggled against him, caught up in her blind panic.

"I need to see Nova. Harry—where's Harry?" She thrashed about, trying to see past him.

"Nova survived the crash, but she had to be cut from the wreck. Carlos flew out and he's looking after her at a local vet hospital until she's in a condition that will allow her to be transported home. He says that she will be fine in the long run but will need some rehabilitation work to get there." Savannah began to calm down, relieved that her horse would be all right. "Harry somehow managed to escape the crash without even a scratch. Y'all were very lucky and I don't think I have ever prayed so hard in my life as I have when I got that phone call from the police. I sent thanks to whatever angel was looking after you that night."

"I was in a car crash," Savannah began slowly.

"Yes, you're lucky to have come out of it with only a broken arm, some bruised ribs and some stitches in your forehead. Oh, and another concussion." Bryce's expression was stern, his nostrils flared as if he was angry with her. "I thought we agreed no more head injuries."

"Are you mad at me? I can't even remember what happened. Did I do something stupid?"

Bryce's face softened and he sighed. "I'm not mad at you. I just don't understand what happened. The witnesses say you didn't even try and slow down. It's like you didn't even see the truck pull out. They think maybe you fell asleep at the wheel."

"But I'm normally a careful driver. Ash is the crazy one. I don't think I fell asleep, but if I didn't, then why didn't I slow down?" None if made sense to her. A truck was kinda a big think to miss. Had she fallen asleep?

"Do you remember anything at all?" Bryce stared intently at her.

She tried to think about the last thing she clearly remembered. "I remember being upset about something Frankie said, but I can't remember what that was." Her brain hurt and she closed her eyes.

"Sweetheart, have a rest. Maybe you'll remember some more when you wake up."

Savannah wanted to take heart in Bryce's reassurance, but doubt niggled in. What happened if she hadn't? Guilt hit her hard. She could have killed Nova and Harry, not to mention someone else and she couldn't even remember. What kind of person was she?

CHAPTER 16

After a couple of days, Bryce was able to take her home. He'd insisted on her staying with him, pointing to the fact he had a fully appointed guest room and it would be easier for him to care for her from the luxury of his penthouse than move into Travis's house. Not to mention he had Bob. Savannah tried insisting that she wasn't that bad now. A bit sore, but nothing she couldn't take care of. If she didn't argue too much, it might have been that she secretly wasn't opposed to being spoiled by Bryce. Well, Bryce and Bob.

Whenever she had a quiet moment, usually when she lay in bed, the thread count of the sheets ridiculously high, the pillows filled with real feathers and the mattress covered in a scandalously soft mattress topper, she tried to remember what happened that night.

Such was the case now. Carlos had called to say Nova would be heading home in a few days and Harry was curled up on her bed snoring. Savannah was beginning to suspect the pup was going through a growth spurt, given how much he was sleeping lately. In the weeks since her accident, the pup hadn't appeared to show any signs of trauma or post traumatic distress, and that went some way to alleviating her guilt. She still couldn't let herself off the hook until she understood what had happened. Bryce had told her that the local police would have a report soon and, hopefully, she would have her answers then.

"How's my patient this morning?" Bryce greeted her with a coffee cup in his hand. She eyed it covetously. Following her gaze, he moved his mug behind his back. "Bob has just brewed a fresh pot and breakfast has been delivered from a little café I like. Well, is it really breakfast still at ten in the morning?"

"I would still be sleeping if Carlos hadn't called and woken me up. Nova will be home soon." Savannah felt relief at being able to say the words. "Anyway, I don't think I've had this many sleep-ins in, well, forever."

He smiled mischievously at her and, before she could ponder what it meant, pulled the toasty warm covers off her. "Well, you're awake now. Come on, up you get."

Grumbling to herself, she followed him out into the living area, the dining table set up with French pastries. Bob stood behind boxes piled high on the kitchen bench. Savannah grabbed a buttery soft croissant and pulled the end off, placing it in her mouth. She closed her eyes to savor the moment, the taste dancing decadently across her palate. When she opened them, she was embarrassed to find Bryce staring at her hungrily. She innocently held the plate of pastries up.

"Hungry for one of these?"

A seductive gleam flowered in his eyes. "I'm hungry, but I don't think it's the croissants that will satisfy me."

Savannah almost spat her food out at him, shocked to her core that he would express his lust so openly. She glanced around to see if Bob had heard, but the butler, being the soul of discretion, appeared to be intent on cleaning a spot on the kitchen counter.

"These are amazing. Which café did you get them from?"

He pulled his gaze away and looked down at his tablet. "I had them flown in from Paris overnight. Oh, and I'm thinking about buying us a yacht."

Savannah's head swam with the quicksilver change in direction the conversation had taken. "I like boats. Something to putt-putt around on the water, just the two of us. Hang on, did you say this"—she waved her croissant around—"was in Paris yesterday?"

"Yes, and the yacht I had in mind might need more than just the two of us to putt-putt around."

"Oh, like a couple of our friends?"

Bryce's generous mouth twitched. Clearly what she said amused him. "More like a crew. And I was thinking about putt-putting around the Greek Isles on it."

Savannah's mouth dropped open. "How big is this thing? It sounds crazy expensive."

"This one has a smaller boat that you drive up inside it, a jacuzzi, pool, a water slide, helipad, and I think it mentioned a dance floor. I believe they're asking a hundred million for it."

Savannah wasn't sure what shocked her the most—the features of the yacht or the calm way he casually threw around a hundred million dollars like it was change. "It seems weird that you're so rich."

"In what way?" He looked up at her, his brow raised questioningly.

"It's just that, most of the time, you're so normal, and then you drop something like a Rolex like it's nothing or, over breakfast, tell me you want to buy a crazy expensive yacht or you have to jet off somewhere on your private plane."

"Money doesn't make me not normal, but it does mean I

get to spoil you. Now finish your breakfast before it goes cold."

Savannah wasn't going to argue with that—not when there was all this calorie laden goodness around.

"I'M SO sorry I didn't call earlier, but I only just found out." Miranda's words came out in a great gush over the phone. "Are you okay?"

"Yeah, I was so lucky. A broken arm and cracked ribs and I'll no longer look identical to Ash, thanks to a scar I'm going to have on my forehead but, overall, not too bad."

"Do you need me to come and help you or do anything? How are Nova and Harry?"

Savannah smiled, gratitude flowing through her at her friend's concern. "Harry's fine, not a scratch. Nova is home now, she's going to need some time to get back on track, but Carlos has had her under UV lights to help with the healing and he just ordered an aqua walker that he's excited to get to use as part of her recovery. He assures me she will be good as new for the next season. In the meantime, Gabi is talking about doing an embryo transfer from her. And don't worry about me. I'm staying at Bryce's and he's taking very good care of me." She couldn't quite keep the smugness that only the truly spoiled got as she looked into the kitchen. "In fact, Bryce is coming home, or should I say, upstairs for lunch."

"Isn't that thoughtful of him. Putting you ahead of work—and it's not the first time either." Savannah wasn't sure why the words made her feel like she'd done something wrong. Maybe it was the tone. Before she could put her finger on it, the moment had passed, and Miranda had moved on. "I'm so glad you're not too badly hurt. When I heard about your crash, my heart dropped. It must have been so scary."

Savannah scratched her neck. "To be honest, I can't actually remember it or most of the day leading up to it."

Miranda gave a little laugh. "Maybe that's a good thing."

"Yeah, I guess. Now tell me all about how you and Ed are going. Do you think you'll be back to the bigger rodeos soon?"

"Some days I think we're going good and then the next we come in last place. It's so frustrating. But I'll see you at Frankie's grand opening no matter what. I think it's going to be a day everyone will remember."

Savannah walked into the living room as she spoke and idly picked up a glass orb. Inside, it looked like the artist had captured fire, encapsulating it for eternity. "I better get going, I can smell lunch is almost ready."

"Okay, see you soon." The phone went dead.

"Mr Dougson bought that from a dear friend—the renowned glass artist, Evelyn Hart—at her first ever exhibition. You might have heard of her?" Savannah jumped. Bob hardly ever spoke to her unless asking about her needs.

Face scrunched, she shook her head. "I've never heard of her."

"Mr Dougson has always had a good eye for making money. I believe it is now worth fifty thousand dollars."

Savannah stared at him, horrified at the value of the fragile piece she held in her hands. Holding her breath, she carefully returned it to its place.

Bob smiled approvingly. "I believe Mr Dougson is on his way up. May I begin to serve your meal?"

She smiled her thanks and took the proffered chair Bob held for her. Her mouth began to water when he brought a tray over with two bowls of steaming soup on it. It had the tell-tale aroma of a Sra Ana special. She'd been telling both Bryce and Sra Ana for the last couple of days that she was feeling better, but who was she to argue if they wanted to keep this up? She took a spoonful—it was delicious, as usual.

Savannah's thoughts drifted back to her conversation with Miranda and she smiled. She couldn't wait to see her friend.

~

"MR DOUGSON, I have a call for you. He says he's from the sheriff's department."

"Thank you, Silvia. I'll take it." Bryce set aside the memo he'd been reading and picked up the handset. "Hello, Bryce speaking."

"Hello, Bryce. How long has it been since we last spoke? Five, ten years?"

"Jimmy, now you're trying to make me feel old. How's the wife?"

"Good. She's taken up watercolors, so that keeps her busy now the kids are at school." There was a pause at the other end of the phone. "I can't imagine you left a message for me to call you about what Maggie's been up to. What can I do for you, Bryce?"

Bryce twirled the pen around his finger, watching the platinum of the barrel shine in the light as it spun. He'd felt uneasy ever since Savannah had had her crash. His gut told him that something wasn't adding up. "I need a favor."

"Is it going to get me kicked off the force?"

He gave a short bark of laughter. "No, nothing like that. Not yet, at least," he corrected. "I want to know the results of the crash forensics for an automobile accident that happened up your way about a month ago."

"I think I might know the one you're interested in. If I remember correctly, there was one that a young gal was involved in. Fell asleep while driving a horse trailer and went into a prime mover."

"That's the one. Can you get a copy sent to me?"

"For a friend, I might be able to find a way for an email to somehow get to you. She must be very important for you to call a favor in."

Bryce didn't know if important began to describe the gut-wrenching fear he'd felt when he'd received the call that Savannah had been in a wreck. If she hadn't come out of it alive … well, he wasn't sure he'd have been able to live without her. He loosened his grip on the handset. "Yeah, you could say that."

CHAPTER 17

The itch was going to drive her nuts. Savannah wiggled her fingers to see if it would ease the itch to no avail. Although her ribs were still aching, she'd insisted she was in a good enough shape to be able to take part in the demonstration for the grand opening. Now she followed Frankie, Gabi and Chloe around as they went through any last-minute details before the big event the next day.

Savannah spied a piece of fencing wire that had been left behind. The importance of listening to the plans for the big demonstration fled before her euphoria. Quickly, she picked it up, holding it in her hands like she'd found the holy grail. This might be the answer to all her itchy problems.

"I think we can really work Savannah's injuries in our favor. What better way to show the results of training and the temperament of the horses we breed than for her to ride them with a cast on her arm, sore ribs, and be doing it bridle-less and bareback?" Trust Gabi to spin a disaster into a PR dream opportunity. "Now, I've organized for Deb, Megan, Joao and Mitch to take turns giving guided tours of the new facilities." Gabi looked back and shook her head in admonishment. "Are you going to keep up, Savannah?"

Savannah stopped her enthusiastic scratching—which had felt like heaven—to find she'd fallen behind. "Sorry, but it was driving me nuts. I wasn't really listening anyway." Chloe laughed at her blunt, honest reply.

"Well, if you've taken care of it now, can you please pay attention?" Gabi really had the despaired teacher voice down pat, Savannah decided, reluctantly parting with her piece of wire.

"Are you sure you want to do that?" Frankie asked. "You don't know when you might need it again, and I wouldn't want you to incur the wrath of Gabi because you were itchy."

Savannah quickly doubled back to collect the discarded wire. Frankie might have a point.

"Now, if I have everyone's attention again, I see catering has just arrived. Mae will be working with him." Savannah was surprised to see it was the same caterer that had been on the film set. She smiled when she noticed that Sra Ana was already there to boss him around. "All the trade stalls will be set up by this evening. Black Angus is obviously the biggest one and will be set up right beside the autograph area. Throughout the day, we will rotate Frankie, Luciano and Joao and then, for one hour only—and personally, I think it will be complete pandemonium—we will have the unannounced surprise appearance of Kirk Cooper and Ash Decker."

Savannah couldn't wait to see her sister. She'd been disappointed when she'd discovered that, due to scheduling conflicts, Ash and Kirk wouldn't be arriving till the morning of the opening.

"Now, if you don't have any questions, I want you all to make sure you're ready for your demonstrations. I need them to run like clockwork." Giving each of them a stern look, Gabi headed over to talk to her mother.

Frankie exasperatedly watched her go and then looked back, shaking her head. "Well, kids, you heard her. Let's go through it one more time."

SAVANNAH LOOKED at the bright blue sky, the finest wispy clouds floating above. It was impossible to feel anything but joy with a day like today. In fact, it was a Goldilocks type of day—not too hot, not too cold, but just right. Like in a fairy tale, she half expected to have some birds settle on her shoulder singing songs. Quick sideways glances proved there were no feathery friends in the vicinity and, giving one final scratch with her wire, she slipped it down inside her cast for later use.

"Savannah!"

She turned expectantly to see her friend rushing toward her, arms outstretched. Awkward with her cast, she still managed to hug Miranda close.

"I'm so glad you could make it." Miranda fairly glowed with excitement. "You look great by the way."

Miranda beamed at her. "Thanks, I'm so excited for today. How are you feeling?"

"I'm good. A tiny bit sore still, but I don't think it will stop me from doing my demonstration with Frankie. I'm going to be riding one of the horses Chloe's been training, since Nova's still out of action."

"That's a shame. It would have been awesome to have Nova and Sampson in the arena at the same time."

Savannah could still remember what it was like the last time her and Frankie had ridden the horses together. "Yeah, it's pretty amazing. And Sampson, well, he's such a magnetic presence, so I think the crowd will still love it."

"I'm sure they will. How's Harry?"

Savannah looked about. The pup had been following her around all morning. "He was here a few minutes ago." A pang of concern hit her stomach, settling into a cold hard lump. "It isn't like him to wander off, maybe he's headed to the house."

"I'm sure he can't have gone too far. Do you want me to help look for him?"

Savannah's stress settled down at her friend's offer. "Yeah, I guess I'll look around here and then head to the house and maybe you could check with Sra Ana and any of the others you see? Maybe they know where he went."

"I'm on it." Miranda dashed away. Savannah began to call Harry's name, listening carefully to hear if he was barking in response. He was usually her shadow and, even if he got distracted by something, he would come running back if he heard his name. Anxiety threatened to overwhelm her the longer she couldn't find him. She was almost in tears when she spied Bryce over at the Black Angus Trade Stall. She bolted over to him. Bryce would know what to do.

He took one look at her face and immediately grew concerned. He gripped her arms tightly. "What happened?"

"I can't find Harry. Have you seen him?" Her voice trembled with fear. "I think something's happened to him."

"He can't have gone too far. I'll head toward the road, just in case he took off that way with all the excitement. You keep looking here." He waited till she nodded and then ran off, calling Harry's name. Savannah took a moment to gather herself, her heart pounding painfully and her stomach feeling sick, and then turned and headed toward the house. He had to be here somewhere.

CHAPTER 18

The sky no longer looked bright and filled with promise, Goldilocks chased away by the bears. Instead, Savannah felt like she was about to start crying. Something bad had happened to Harry, she could feel it. There was no other possible explanation for his absence. Her throat burned as the tears started to fall down her cheeks.

"Savannah! Come quick!" Miranda came bolting out from behind some parked cars. "I've found him."

Savannah wiped her eyes, eagerly looking around for him, "Harry, come on boy," she called. Confused, she looked at Miranda. "Where is he?"

"That's what I was just about to tell you. He won't come to me when I call him and, when I tried to catch him, he ran off. You'll have to come and get him."

"He must be really scared with all the commotion to act like that. It's just so unlike him. He knows you."

"I tried. I spent ages trying to get him and he kept running off. That's when I decided it was going to be quickest if I just came back and got you."

Savannah felt almost dizzy with relief. Thank goodness

Harry had been found and was safe—or at least would be as soon as she went and got him. "Show me where he is."

Miranda turned and headed back the way she had come from. "He's over here." Quickly, Savannah followed, close on her heels. *Don't go anywhere, Harry. I'm on my way.*

THE RING of the phone caused Bryce to jump, smashing his head on the wheel guard of the trailer he'd been peering under. Cussing, he rubbed his sore skull as he answered the phone.

"Bad timing?" Officer Warren asked on the other end.

"How are you at finding missing dogs?"

"Can't say that's much of a specialty for me and, more than likely, it's out of my jurisdiction. Look, I thought you might want to hear about this as soon as I found out. I tracked down the forensics on that crash you were after and I don't think that gal fell asleep at all."

Bryce stilled, his entire being focused on the voice on the other end of the phone. "What do you mean?"

"The brake line was partially cut, but only enough to allow the brake fluid to gradually drip out. Whoever did it didn't want them to fail straightaway."

"You're sure they were cut?" Bryce could feel the blood beginning to pound in his ears. If it was true, then the accident added to all the other strange things that had been happening to Savannah meant she was in grave danger.

"I'm sure. Look, I've sent through the report. You can read it for yourself, it's all in there."

Quickly, Bryce hung up the phone, dialing Savannah's number. He went cold when it went straight to voicemail. Desperately, he began to call her name, running back in the direction that he'd last seen her headed.

Luciano came running up. "What is wrong?"

Bryce grabbed him by the arms, the worry making him frantic. "Have you seen Savannah?"

"No, not since she left with her friend to find the dog."

"Where did they go?" His palms were slick with sweat where they gripped the big Brazilian.

"I did not see. Is she okay?" The terror now shone from Luciano's face, his pupils dilated—terror that he was sure was reflected in his own.

"I don't know, but I have to find her."

"I'll get the others and we'll split up. Don't worry, my friend. We will find her."

Bryce let go of the other man and sprung away. "I just hope we're in time."

TERROR BLINDED him as he frantically dashed from person to person, demanding to know if they'd seen Savannah. From time to time, he would see one of the others out of the corner of his eye doing the same. At last, he had a breakthrough when someone thought they'd seen two red-haired women headed toward the stand of trees near the boundary fence. Without thanks, he took off in the direction they'd pointed. His breath rasped, the muscles in his legs burning as he pushed his body past it limits.

Hold on, Savannah. I'm coming.

CHAPTER 19

"Are you sure he's out here?" Savannah pushed a branch out of her way, a jittery feeling skittering around in her belly. It was getting close to Frankie and Luciano cutting the ribbon and then the demonstrations would begin. She desperately wanted to find Harry but, at the same time, she was beginning to stress about her other obligations. "Surely he hasn't come this far. Maybe he's already headed back and is looking for me." Savannah began to turn, preparing to leave the way she'd come.

"I wouldn't do that if I was you." Miranda's voice held a deadly menace. Confused, Savannah glanced at her friend over her shoulder. Horrified, she stopped dead in her tracks. Miranda stood, looking like she meant business, a handgun aimed directly at Savannah.

Savannah shook her head, bewildered at the circumstances she now found herself in. A strange paralysis settled over her. Except for her head, her body felt frozen. "Miranda, what's going on?"

"You know, we were friends. Do you know how long it's been since I had a real friend?" Miranda's skin was flushed, sweat breaking out on her forehead. "But then he had to come along and ruin it all."

Savannah stared at her, astonished and very much aware of the gun still aimed in her direction. She swallowed and attempted to smile—anything to calm the situation down. But it felt like she was in a fog as she tried to process Miranda's words. "Are you talking about Bryce? Miranda, we're still friends. In fact, I don't think I would've gotten through being on the road after Ash left if it hadn't been for you. No guy is going to get between us. It's silly to be jealous."

"Jealous? Jealous!" Miranda's voice was shrill, and for the first time, Savannah began to consider that her friend was becoming mentally unhinged. "Hardly. But why did it have to be him? Anyone else and it wouldn't have had to come to this." Savannah watched nervously, her heart pounding as Miranda agitatedly waved the gun around. "But it did come to this. So keep walking." She gestured with the gun to precede her and continue the way they'd been heading.

"Miranda, I'm going with you. You don't need to point a gun at me." Without thinking, Savannah's hand sought out the diamond pendant she wore around her neck as she tried to remain calm.

The other woman's eyes went wild. Angrily stalking forward, she ripped the necklace from Savannah's throat and contemptuously threw it to the ground. "Since I'm the one with the gun, I'd say that makes me in charge. Now get moving." Pulse racing, not knowing what else to do, Savannah meekly complied.

BRYCE'S BREATH came out in short, ragged gasps, his legs like jelly. He promised himself that, when he got Savannah back with him safe and sound, he was going to hit the gym and get in shape. Once he reached the tree line, he could see where it looked like someone had recently gone through, the branches broken and bent. Slowing his pace, he cautiously entered, every sense tingling. It was dimmer in the trees, except for broken rays of light that managed to penetrate the canopy. It was sheer dumb luck that a glint caught his attention. Looking down, he let out an anguished cry when he found the pink diamond pendant he'd given Savannah. A grim determination pushed back the terror. He was close, and whoever had Savannah was going to pay.

Over his boiling bloodlust pounding in his ears, he heard a raised woman's voice. Miranda! Was Miranda in trouble too? He needed to calm himself. None of this made sense. The one thing he was certain about was that charging in would only make matters worse. He needed to come up with a plan. Cautiously, he inched his way forward.

CHAPTER 20

Savannah let out a gasp as her foot snagged on the tree root. Propelled forward by a push from behind, she stumbled into the clearing. Her breathing quick and shallow, it felt like she couldn't suck in enough oxygen. Straightening up, her eyes locked on the rectangular hole that had been dug in the center of the clearing. She froze, rooted to the spot. There was no mistaking that it was a grave. Horrified, she clutched at her throat. Remembering she no longer wore her pendant, the reassurance she sought not there, she let her hand drop uselessly to her side.

"You don't have to do this," Savannah pleaded, her voice quivery as her mouth trembled.

"I don't want to do this. I never wanted to do any of it. But he made me. You made me." Miranda's face was a mask of hatred.

"I don't understand."

"It's too late, Savannah. You should've stayed away from him. I'll make it quick. I care enough about you to at least do that for you."

The whites of her eyes showing, Miranda looked wild

and crazy as she aimed the gun again. Petrified, Savannah squeezed her eyes shut, silently farewelling Ash and Bryce as tears streamed down her face. The sharp snap of a branch made her eyes fly open. Miranda closed the distance between them, wrapping an arm around her throat, and pressed the gun hard against Savannah's temple. Savannah whimpered, spots dancing in front of her eyes.

"Whoever is out there better show themselves and come out where I can see you. Nice and slow, hands up, or I'll shoot her."

Bryce stepped carefully out from behind a tree, his hands outstretched high above his head. "I'm doing what you're saying. How about we all calm down?"

"You," snarled Miranda in Savannah's ear, making her jump, the gun digging harder into her. "I don't know why I didn't plan for you to be here to see this. It's perfect." Miranda's voice had gone syrupy sweet.

"You're the one who cut the brake lines." Bryce's hard stare was unwavering, no hint of doubt to his statement.

Miranda agitatedly swung the gun around. "I didn't want her to suffer. I thought it would be quick." Savannah froze. It didn't make sense. What brake lines? She sucked in a breath, her heart palpitating in her chest when she realized how perilously close she was to the freshly dug grave. The blood beating in her ears almost made her miss the continued exchange between the others.

"Did you have anything to do with the things going missing?" It was clear Bryce was fitting the pieces of the puzzle together.

"I wanted to scare her. I still hoped that maybe she would break up with you, but she always ran to you when something went wrong. It was after you stayed with us for a while that I knew there was nothing I could do to save her." A chill rocked Savannah to her core at the matter-of-fact way

Miranda said it. "I almost thought I'd done it, too, when I injected Nova with Procaine. Did you ever know it's in penicillin and it's perfectly safe as long as you use it intramuscularly? But I think you saw the results for yourself if you inject it in a vein." It was freaky how Miranda had switched gears and was now in teacher mode.

"But why? I don't understand why you would want to do that to me. And Nova could have gotten seriously hurt." If she was going to die, Savannah wanted to know what crime, what horrible act she had committed to deserve it.

"I didn't want to do it to you. But unfortunately, I had no other choice. I wanted to make him suffer."

"But why?" Still Savannah persisted. "You keep saying it's because of Bryce, but what did he do?"

Bryce peered at Miranda closer, shock marching across his face. "I don't know why I never saw it before. There are similarities between the two of you."

"Lily was my half-sister, my older sister. I loved her so much and you took her from me!" Miranda screamed, her arm tightening around Savannah's throat setting the black spots to dancing in front of her eyes again. "But you never loved her, did you? She was just a convenience for you when you had time for her. How does it feel to know Savannah is going to die because of you?"

Bryce looked like he'd been punched in the gut, his repentance palatable as he bowed under its weight. Through the stupor of terror that engulfed Savannah, the sight of Bryce put low by guilt that wasn't his to shoulder broke her. Slowly, she raised her chin, lifting her eyes. She put all her love and forgiveness in that single look.

"You aren't to blame for this, Bryce."

Bryce straightened at her words, their gazes locking, love and anguish swirling between them. He tore his eyes away, directing the force of his appeal to Miranda. "I cared about her. I never wished anything bad to happen to Lily. I'm so sorry for what happened, but if someone deserves to be punished, it's me. Savannah is your friend. Let her go, and you can do whatever you want with me."

"No, that's not going to work. Then you wouldn't feel anything. I want you to live with the pain of knowing what it's like to lose someone you love—someone you really care about—because you never cared about my sister. Your life just continued as if nothing ever happened. People always saying how generous and great you were. Always in magazines and giving money to charities like you're this awesome human being." Savannah could hear Miranda edging closer to insanity. She pitied her, the pain she'd felt at the loss of her sister and, over all those years, the resentment and hatred she'd felt toward Bryce. She watched as Bryce, seeing Miranda distracted with her rant, inched closer.

An itch in her arm made her twitch and then, in a stupendous wave of hope, Savannah remembered the piece of fencing wire she'd slipped in there earlier. Slowly, she crept her free hand along her cast, her fingers tantalizing close. Inch by inch, she slid the wire free. From the corner of her eye, she could see they were less than a foot away from the edge of the grave. Bryce continued to slowly close the distance between them.

Miranda, at last seeing how close he'd crept, took a step backwards, dangerously close to the edge. Feeling the earth start to give way under her weight, she pushed against Savannah. Seeing her opportunity, Savannah dug the wire into Miranda's leg, twisting it. Her captor let out a screech of pain and frustration and, taking a step back to free herself, she overstepped and the dirt gave way.

Desperately, Miranda clutched at Savannah as she lost her balance and fell backwards, dragging her down with her. The last thing Savannah saw was Bryce leaping forward, terror-stricken, hands outstretched to save her, and then everything swirled around her. They both landed heavily, pain ratcheting from Savannah's barely-healed ribs. Stunned, she lie there, the world around her retreating, a peacefulness pulling her into its reassuring embrace.

It took a few moments for Savannah to comprehend that the grip around her neck was slack. Horrified and fearing the worst for Miranda, Savannah awkwardly rolled over, her cast making it difficult. Bryce was ashen-faced and breathing heavily as he jumped down into the grave.

"Please tell me she's all right," pleaded Savannah.

"I'm not sure if that's the first thing I was worried about," Bryce muttered, leaning over to take Miranda's pulse before quickly locating and removing the gun.

"The Miranda that did this isn't the Miranda I know."

"I think you'll find that the Miranda you thought you knew never existed." Bryce took off his belt and wrapped it around the unconscious woman's hands, securing them tightly. Satisfied that she wouldn't be able to cause any more trouble, he pulled Savannah roughly into his embrace, kissing her face all over as if to make certain she was unharmed. "I don't know what I would've done if anything had happened to you." His pain cut through Savannah like a knife.

She took his face between her hands. "But nothing did. Now get me out of this grave before I completely freak out."

He lifted her out easily and took a few steps to the edge of the clearing. Still cradling her gently in his arms, he lowered himself down. Tenderly, he brushed the dirt from her face, the action unlocking the dam that held back the shock and horror of her ordeal, and she began to cry uncontrollably.

"I'm so sorry, Savannah. If you'll let me, I'll spend the rest of my life making this up to you. I'm so sorry," Bryce said brokenly, his face buried in her hair.

Spent, Savannah sniffled. "It wasn't your fault, none of it ever was. Miranda obviously had issues, and Lily, well, she didn't have to do what she did either. She made that choice, not you."

His body shuddered against her as if releasing all the guilt he'd carried around for so long. "I never thought I would be free from her memory."

Savannah gingerly turned to face Bryce, her ribs still aching painfully. She leaned forward until her forehead touched his. "You're free now." He nodded, acknowledging the truth of her words. He gently gathered her into his arms and kissed her. Savannah closed her eyes, the love for this wounded cowboy impossible to escape. "I love you, Bryce."

"I don't deserve your love." Savannah's heart clenched painfully. "But I'm eternally grateful that you do. Everything I have, I'd give up tomorrow if you asked me. Savannah, I love you."

Savannah wasn't sure how long they remained holding each other and healing. Slowly, growling and cussing drew her attention away from Bryce. "I think Miranda's awake."

"Unfortunately. I'd better call the police."

Suddenly, a whimper sounded from out in the trees. "Did you hear that?" Excited, she bounded to her feet, a move she immediately regretted when pain from her ribs made her wince.

"I think I did." Bryce reached out a hand to steady her. Together, they followed the noise until they found the source tied tightly to a tree, a rag bounding his mouth shut. Bryce quickly untied it, and the pup squirmed about, wiggling and trying to climb onto Savannah's lap. Although thirsty, Harry otherwise appeared unharmed. Savannah was grateful that, even in her delusions, Miranda hadn't hurt her pup.

"I guess I'd better make that call to the police now," Bryce said, pulling a phone from his pocket.

"Can you ask that they take Miranda into custody discreetly? I don't want Frankie and Luciano's big day overshadowed by this."

Bryce smiled at her fondly, kissing the top of her head. "I love you. Only you would worry about that after everything you've been through today."

The words made Savannah's insides turn to mush. "Well, it's an important day for them," she defended herself.

"After this, I'm buying that superyacht and we're spending a month—no, two—laying under the Greek sun and recuperating. I think this cowgirl deserves a bit of spoiling that only a billionaire can provide."

Savannah blinked at him in shock. "Hang on, what? A billionaire? I mean, I knew money wasn't an issue, but billionaire?"

Bryce looked at her innocently, as if unsure what all the fuss was about. "I'm sure I mentioned it."

"Ah, no. It's not the kind of thing I'm likely to forget."

He looked intently at her, his heart looking at her through the window of his eyes. "Does it make any difference?"

She smiled at him, her cowgirl's billionaire. "Not in the least. Now give me a kiss, I've never been kissed by a billionaire before."

He pulled her close, his proximity sending little shivers through her. "I've been a billionaire the whole time."

"Are you going to keep arguing, or are you going to kiss me?"

Bryce lowered his head, kissing her until she was breathless. Her broken cowboy was whole again and, thrilled by his closeness, she surrendered to the kisses of her cowgirl's billionaire.

*I*t was hard to believe another year had almost come to a close. But it seemed that way most years, Sra Ana conceded as she added the finishing touches to her turkey. It had been almost forty years since she had first met her love—her soul mate—Eduardo. In her mind, she still saw him as he was, his young man's body once again strong and lean, his luscious locks inky black. Her breathless young girl's love had matured into something deeper, a love that was as natural to her as each breath she drew in.

She smiled at the memories and, finally satisfied that the bird had been done to perfection, she gathered it up and walked proudly into the dining room. The table was laden with food, and pride of place in front of Senhor Eduardo, a free space for him to do the honors of carving the turkey. From the open door, she could see into the living room beyond, the Christmas tree now having been relieved of its burden of gifts below. Her husband, seeing her enter, smiled, the crinkles around his eyes now deep caverns, a story to each of them, each one deeply loved. She set the turkey before him, his hand creeping up to hold hers where she rested it on his shoulder.

Deep contentment filled Sra Ana as she looked around the room. Her son, Carlos, no longer a toddling little boy, but now a fine strapping man with a dark-haired little boy of his own, sat beside his wife, Megan, his arm proudly around her as always. Her fierce little Gabriella had harnessed her passions and looked set to rule the world if they weren't careful. Joao, her husband, son of Sra Ana's beloved best friend, sat with their baby daughter, Maria Ana, in his arms. Her heart overflowed as she looked at the rest of her family, such gifts she'd never expected.

Gracie, the first of her adopted grandbabies, now a big girl of nine, sat to one side of her parents, Deb and Mitch, so she could be next to her best friend, Teeny. Who, in turn, sat next to her father, Travis, and stepmom, Chloe. The two girls giggled as they chatted away as only young girls can do.

Sra Ana smiled lovingly at Frankie, the first of her Australian adopted daughters, the one who none of them would've been there without. The beautiful blonde held her toddler daughter, Harper, on her lap while her doting husband, Luciano, bounced the other twin—his son— Luciano Jnr, while he laughed at something Kirk had said across the table.

Kirk's wife, Ash, was having a heated conversation with her twin, Savannah, judging from the gestures and animated expressions of the auburn-haired girls. Savannah's husband, Bryce, indulgently watching on.

Her eyes sparkled with unshed tears, the nostalgia bitter-sweet. Sra Ana was so very proud of the family her and Eduardo had created. Her smile quavered as she glanced down at her husband, noticing now that only silver remained where there had once been the deepest of black. She took her seat beside him.

"We really did create paradise, didn't we?"

He leaned over and gave her a gentle kiss on the temple. "I never had any doubts, my love."

Sra Ana had never asked for more than what she had been given, but somehow, she'd ended up with more than she'd ever known she needed. Silently, she raised her glass in salute. Her husband, holding her gaze with a loving look, joined her toast. "A paradise found."

Senhor Eduardo clinked his glass to hers. "To our bull rider's paradise."

THE END

As an Indie Author, reviews help me get my books noticed. If you enjoyed reading Savannah's story as much as I did writing it, please leave a review. It will make all the difference to me

If you loved, *A Cowgirl's Billionaire,* sign up for my newsletter to get updates on new releases as well as exclusive extras.

Now, turn the page to discover the Billionaire Hearts Ranch, beginning with Colt.

SNEAK PEEK - THE WOUNDED COWBOY BILLIONAIRE (BOOK 1, BILLIONAIRE HEARTS RANCH)

The sky was clean and bright, barely a cloud in the sky as Colt swung the rope experimentally, warming up as he walked his horse around. The cute cowgirl coming the other way recognized him, her eyes widening gratifyingly and her gaze dropping to take in his gleaming gold world champion buckle. He sent her his best slow and lazy smile, cocking his head as he appraised her appreciatively. Colt promised himself that he would catch up with her later and get to know her better.

It was a good day to be alive. Big Wheels, his horse, was calm and steady beneath him, too much of an old rodeo hand to be bothered with nerves. A movement at the edge of the warmup area caught his attention. Standing to her full five-foot three inches high, his sister waved, pausing to see if he'd noticed her before setting off waving again. Beside Indie, standing tall, was one of his best friends—her fiancé—Bennett. Grinning at them, he loped Big Wheels over.

"I didn't expect to see you guys here. I hope someone's looking after my ranch."

Indie cocked her head at him. "The ranch is fine. Maybe

we just wanted to come and spend some time with you. You know, live the playboy billionaire lifestyle. Don't think I didn't see you checking out all the pretty girls." She looked up at Bennett, a silly smile on her face. "Can we just tell him already?"

Bennett's smile was just as goofy. "If you don't, I will."

"Is someone going to tell me? Why didn't you just call me if you had something to say?" His sister looked like she was about to explode with whatever news she had to tell. Maybe he should torment her a little longer, string it out. Really, what kind of big brother wouldn't take advantage of this situation?

"We didn't want to tell you over the phone. This is something that I wanted to see your face when we told you. You're the only family I have, and I want to do this right."

"You guys didn't run off and get married, did you? Bennett, you and I are going to have words if you didn't give my little sister the big wedding she's always dreamed of."

Bennet exchanged a knowing look with him. "You think she'd let me get away with an elopement?"

Colt chuckled. "Maybe not. So, what's this big news you're all fired up to tell me about?"

Indie's eyes shimmered with excitement and she clutched at Bennett's arm as if to anchor herself and not get carried away with her emotions. "Colt, I'm pregnant. We're going to be having a baby." Colt felt like he'd been poleaxed. His baby sister was going to have a baby. A bittersweet wave hit him. *Mom would have loved being a grandma.* "You're happy for us, aren't you, Colt?" Indie's eyes no longer shimmered with excitement. Now tears threatened, a storm on the horizon.

"You caught me by surprise, but I like the idea of being Uncle Colt." He slid off his horse and wrapped her up in a giant bear hug. "You're going to make the best mom," he whispered in her ear.

He shook Bennett's hand. "Congratulations. I'm over the moon for you guys."

Bennett's grip was firm. "Thanks. You know I'll make sure they never want for anything."

"If I'd had my doubts, I wouldn't have let you anywhere near her when we were in high school." Colt's name crackled over the loudspeaker. "I'm next in. Are you guys staying around?"

"Yeah, this one here"—Bennett smiled lovingly down at Indie—"informed me that she already has cravings. So, we'll stay for the rodeo and then head home afterwards."

Indie punched her fiancé lightly on the arm. "Hey, mister, these cravings are real. Now enough with this chitchat. Colt, go catch a steer, and you"—she crooked her finger at Bennett —"need to go hunt me down some pickles, corndogs and ice cream."

"That seems fair enough," Colt said, climbing back into the saddle.

"She plans on eating them all together like one big, pickle corndog sundae." Bennett shuddered at the thought.

Colt grimaced, staring in horror at his sister. "Indie, that's gross."

"And I don't care, now git." She shooed him away with her hands. Colt could feel a gooey smile on his face. Well, how about that? His baby sister was having a baby, and with one of his best friends, no less.

ACKNOWLEDGMENTS

A debt of gratitude to my editor Rebekah Groves for her patience with me.

Another big thanks to Megan from Designed with Grace for her cover design. Who knew it was so hard to get pictures of hot cowboys that were wearing shirts.

Buy Now

A cowgirl's movie star

A fiery cowgirl with big dreams. A movie star far from home. When their two worlds collide, will their love be strong enough to hold them together or will they be pulled apart

Buy Now

A cowgirl's billionaire

A cowgirl adrift. A broken billionaire cowboy. Can he free himself from the past to be the man she needs now?

Buy Now

Cowboy Christmas Series

The Mistletoe Collection

Boots and Mistletoe

Cowboy boots, mistletoe, and a holiday do-over…

Buy Now

The Cowboy Under the Mistletoe

Mistletoe and the Billionaire's Cowgirl

Billionaire Hearts Ranch Series

February 2021 Release

The wounded cowboy billionaire

The cowboy's billionairess

The billionaire's cowgirl

The cowgirl's fake billionaire marriage

A cowboy's riches (Prequel)

ABOUT THE AUTHOR

Edith MacKenzie or Eddie Mac to her friends is an author of sweet and wholesome contemporary cowboy romance. They say in literary circles to write what you know, and Eddie has certainly taken that to heart. Before embarking on a writing career, she trained horses professionally and brings that wealth of knowledge to her writing.

Now a mum to a boy and girl, as well as wife, she delights with her tales of strong cowgirls and their adventures in finding love. When not weaving the love stories of her characters, she enjoys hanging out with her family and animals, as well as reading, fishing and camping.

Just remember—once a cowgirl, always a cowgirl.

instagram.com/edith_mackenzie_author

amazon.com/Edith-MacKenzie

bookbub.com/profile/edith-mackenzie

facebook.com/EddieMacAuthor

GLOSSARY OF AUSSIE SLANG

Now everyone knows that cobbers from the Land Down Under speak the Queen's English, but if you don't know to Tracky Daks from your Servo, I've put together a quick little cheat sheet.

A few kangaroos loose in the top paddock - To not be working with all of your mental capacity, to be a bit daft

A few stubbies short of a six pack - Crazy

Ankle Bitter - Small child

Arvo - Afternoon

Aussie Salute - wave flies away

Bail - to cancel plans

Belly Up - Go out of business

Blind - Intoxicated

Bloody - Very. Used to extenuate a point

Bloody oath - Yes or its true

Bludger - Someone who is lazy

Buggered - Exhausted

Buggie Smugglers - Speedos, swimming trunks

Cactus - Die

Can't be bothered - Not in a mood to do anything

Cark it - Die

Choccy Bikkie - Chocolate cookie

Clucky - Feeling maternal

Crook - Feeling sick

Daks - Trousers e.g. Tracky Daks are tracksuit pants

Dog's breakfast - Messy (does not relate to food), a bit of a shambles

Dry as a dead dingo's doing - Exceptionally dry

Fair Go - Give someone a chance

Flat out like a lizard drinking' - Not doing very much at all

Going off like a frog in a blender - Going off by itself can be good e.g. the surf was going off - it was good surf conditions. If Going off is added to anything else it is bad, in this case you can imagine what a frog in a blender would feel like

Good on ya - Good for you (sarcastic)

Go Troppo - To lose the plot, go crazy

Grog - Alcohol

Have a barney - To have a tiff or blue

Hit the frog and toad - Hit the road, get going

Idiot Box - TV

Jumper - Sweater

Man's not a camel - A man gets thirsty and would indeed like the beverage you are offering him

Mate - Friend or conversely could be someone you barely know

Mate's Rates - To get a large discount because you are friends

Nay, Yeah - Yes

Pull the wool over someone's eyes - To trick or mislead someone

Reckon - For sure

Ripsnorter - Can also be interchanged with beaut, bonza. Someone doing something exceptionally good

Servo - Petrol Station

Shout - To pay for the next round of drinks

Six one way, half a dozen the other - Undecided

Sparrow Fart - Before the crack of dawn. Very, very early in the morning

Spit the dummy - To throw a tantrum. A similar display of when an infant spits out their pacifier "dummy" and bursts into a hysterical crying fit.

Stone the flamin' crow - An utterance of surprise of annoyance

Struth - God's truth. Used to express surprise or dismay

She'll be right - Everything is going to okay

Tell 'em they're dreaming - Is never in a million years going to happen

Tighter than a fish's bum - Said person is very frugal with their money

To blow smoke up someone's bum - To give praise that might make the other person cocky or overly confident

Two Pot Screamer - Someone that is a cheap drunk and can not hold their alcohol very well

Up yourself - Stuck up

Ute - Pickup Truck

Whinge - Complain

Whoop whoop - Middle of nowhere

Wrap ya laughing gear 'round that - Eat this

Yarn - To talk or tell tall tales

Yeah, nay - No

You bloody ripper - Very good, a job well done